TRANSMISSION

(THE INVASION CHRONICLES -- BOOK 1)

MORGAN RICE

Books by Morgan Rice

THE INVASION CHRONICLES
TRANSMISSION (Book #1)
ARRIVAL (Book #2)

THE WAY OF STEEL
ONLY THE WORTHY (Book #1)

A THRONE FOR SISTERS
A THRONE FOR SISTERS (Book #1)
A COURT FOR THIEVES (Book #2)
A SONG FOR ORPHANS (Book #3)
A DIRGE FOR PRINCES (Book #4)
A JEWEL FOR ROYALS (BOOK #5)
A KISS FOR QUEENS (BOOK #6)
A CROWN FOR ASSASSINS (Book #7)

OF CROWNS AND GLORY
SLAVE, WARRIOR, QUEEN (Book #1)
ROGUE, PRISONER, PRINCESS (Book #2)
KNIGHT, HEIR, PRINCE (Book #3)
REBEL, PAWN, KING (Book #4)
SOLDIER, BROTHER, SORCERER (Book #5)
HERO, TRAITOR, DAUGHTER (Book #6)
RULER, RIVAL, EXILE (Book #7)
VICTOR, VANQUISHED, SON (Book #8)

KINGS AND SORCERERS
RISE OF THE DRAGONS (Book #1)
RISE OF THE VALIANT (Book #2)
THE WEIGHT OF HONOR (Book #3)
A FORGE OF VALOR (Book #4)
A REALM OF SHADOWS (Book #5)
NIGHT OF THE BOLD (Book #6)

THE SORCERER'S RING
A QUEST OF HEROES (Book #1)
A MARCH OF KINGS (Book #2)
A FATE OF DRAGONS (Book #3)

A CRY OF HONOR (Book #4)
A VOW OF GLORY (Book #5)
A CHARGE OF VALOR (Book #6)
A RITE OF SWORDS (Book #7)
A GRANT OF ARMS (Book #8)
A SKY OF SPELLS (Book #9)
A SEA OF SHIELDS (Book #10)
A REIGN OF STEEL (Book #11)
A LAND OF FIRE (Book #12)
A RULE OF QUEENS (Book #13)
AN OATH OF BROTHERS (Book #14)
A DREAM OF MORTALS (Book #15)
A JOUST OF KNIGHTS (Book #16)
THE GIFT OF BATTLE (Book #17)

THE SURVIVAL TRILOGY
ARENA ONE: SLAVERSUNNERS (Book #1)
ARENA TWO (Book #2)
ARENA THREE (Book #3)

VAMPIRE, FALLEN
BEFORE DAWN (Book #1)

THE VAMPIRE JOURNALS
TURNED (Book #1)
LOVED (Book #2)
BETRAYED (Book #3)
DESTINED (Book #4)
DESIRED (Book #5)
BETROTHED (Book #6)
VOWED (Book #7)
FOUND (Book #8)
RESURRECTED (Book #9)
CRAVED (Book #10)
FATED (Book #11)
OBSESSED (Book #12)

CHAPTER ONE

Kevin was pretty sure you shouldn't be told you were dying when you were thirteen. There probably wasn't a good time to be told it, to be fair, but definitely not when you were thirteen.

"Kevin," Dr. Markham said, leaning forward in his chair, "do you understand what I'm saying to you? Do you have any questions? Do *you*, Ms. McKenzie?"

Kevin looked over to his mom, hoping she would have more of an idea what to say next than he did. Hoping that maybe he'd misheard all of it, and she would explain. She was short and slender, with the tough look of someone who had worked hard to raise her son alone in Walnut Creek, California. Kevin was already taller than she was, and once, just once, she'd said that he looked just like his father.

Right now, she looked as though she was trying to hold back tears.

"Are you sure this isn't a mistake?" she asked. "We only came in to the doctor's because of the things Kevin was seeing."

The things he was seeing. That was such a gentle way to put it, as if even talking about all of it might make it worse, or bring more of it. When Kevin had first told his mother about it, she'd stared at him and then told him he should ignore it. Finally, when he fainted, he'd woken up to find that he had an appointment with the family doctor.

They'd quickly gone from the doctor's office to the hospital for tests, and then to Dr. Markham's office, which was white-walled and filled with mementos of what seemed like trips to every corner of the planet. When Kevin had first stepped in there, he'd felt as though it was an attempt to make a cold, clinical space seem homey. Now he thought maybe Dr. Markham liked to be reminded that there was life that didn't include telling people they were dying.

"Hallucinations can be a factor when it comes to diseases like this," Dr. Markham said, in a careful tone.

Hallucinations didn't seem like the right way to put it, to Kevin. That made it sound as though they were unreal, ghostly things, but the things he saw seemed to fill the world when they came. Images of landscapes he hadn't seen, hints of horizons.

And, of course, the numbers.

1

"23h 06m 29.283s, −05° 02′ 28.59," he said. "It must mean something. It has to."

Dr. Markham shook his head. "I'm sure it must feel that way, Kevin. I'm sure that you must want it all to mean something, but right now, I need you to understand what is happening to you."

That had been part of why Kevin had told his mom about it in the first place. It had taken him weeks to convince her that he wasn't joking, or playing some game. She'd been sure that he wasn't serious at first. When he'd started to have the headaches, she'd taken it more seriously, letting him stay home from school for the day when the pain was paralyzing. When he'd collapsed the first time, she'd rushed him to the doctor.

"What is happening to me?" Kevin asked. The strange thing was how calm he felt—well, not calm. Maybe more kind of numb. Numb was probably the right word for it. His mom looked as though she was on the verge of falling apart, but for Kevin, all of it seemed far away, still waiting to rush in.

"You have one of a group of degenerative brain disorders known as leukodystrophies," Dr. Markham said. "Here, I'll write it down if you like."

"But I've never heard of that before," Kevin's mom said, in the tone of someone for whom that meant it couldn't be real. He could see the tears she was trying to fight back. "How can my son have something I've never even heard of?"

Seeing his mom like that was probably the hardest part of it for Kevin. She'd always been so strong. He'd never had a problem she hadn't been able to solve. He suspected that was what she was thinking too.

"It's a very rare illness, Ms. McKenzie," Dr. Markham said. "Or rather, a collection of illnesses, each of which presents differently. There are different forms, each one caused by a genetic abnormality that affects the white matter, what we call the myelin sheath, of the brain. There are usually only a few hundred sufferers of each of these illnesses at any one time."

"If you know what causes them, can't you do something?" Kevin's mother asked. "Isn't there some gene therapy or something?"

Kevin had seen his mom on the Internet. Now, he guessed he knew what she'd been looking at. She hadn't said anything, but maybe she'd been hoping she was wrong. Maybe she'd been hoping there was something she'd missed.

"There are therapies available for some forms of leukodystrophy," Dr. Markham said. He shook his head. "And we have hope that in the future, they might help, but Kevin's isn't one where there is any established treatment. The sad truth is, the rarer the disease, the less research has been done on it, because the less funding there is for that research."

"There must be something," his mother said. "Some experimental option, some study…"

Kevin reached out to put his hand over his mother's. It was strange that they were already almost the same size.

"It's okay, Mom," he said, trying to sound as if he had everything under control.

"No, it isn't." His mom looked as though she might burst apart with the shock of it all. "If there's nothing, then what do we do next?"

"We use the treatments that are available to give Kevin the best quality of life we can," Dr. Markham said. "For the time that he still has left. I'm sorry, I wish I had better news."

Kevin watched his mother forcing herself to be brave, piecing herself back together a little at a time. He could tell that she was doing it for his sake, and almost felt guilty that she had to.

"What does that mean?" she asked. "What exactly are you proposing to do for Kevin?"

"I'm going to prescribe tablets to help manage the pain," Dr. Markham said, "and to reduce the chances of seizures. Kevin, I know that hallucinations can be distressing, so I'd like you to talk to someone about techniques for managing them, and your responses to them."

"You want Kevin to see a psychologist?" his mother asked.

"Linda Yalestrom is an expert in helping people, particularly young people, to cope with the symptoms that rare illnesses like this can cause," Dr. Markham said. "I strongly recommend that you take Kevin to see her, given the things he has been seeing."

"They're not just hallucinations," Kevin insisted. He was sure that they were more than that.

"I'm sure it must feel that way," Dr. Markham said. "Dr. Yalestrom might be able to help."

"Whatever… whatever you think is best," Kevin's mother said. Kevin could see that she wanted nothing other than to get out of there. There was something he needed to know, though. Something obvious that he felt he should probably ask, even if he didn't really want to hear the answer.

"How long?" he asked. "I mean, how long until I… die?"

That was still a hard word to believe. Kevin found himself hoping it would all turn out to be a mistake, even now, but he knew that it wasn't. It couldn't be.

"It's impossible to say for certain," Dr. Markham said. "The rate of progression for leukodystrophies can vary, while each case is different."

"How long?" Kevin repeated.

"Perhaps six months." Dr. Markham spread his hands. "I'm sorry, Kevin. I can't be more exact than that."

***

Kevin and his mother went home, his mom driving with the kind of care that came when someone knew they would probably fall apart if they didn't concentrate completely. For most of the journey out toward the suburbs, they were silent. Kevin wasn't sure what he could say.

His mother spoke first. "We'll find something," she said. "We'll find another doctor, get a second opinion. We'll try whatever treatment they can think of."

"You can't afford that," Kevin said. His mother worked hard at her job at a marketing agency, but their house was a small one, and Kevin knew there wasn't a lot of money for extra things. He tried not to ask for much, because it only made his mother feel sad when she couldn't give it to him. He hated seeing his mother like that, which only made this harder.

"Do you think any of it matters to me?" his mother demanded. Kevin could see the tears pouring from her eyes now. "You're my son, and you're dying, and... I can't... I can't save you."

"You don't have to save me," Kevin said, although he wished that someone would right then. He wished that someone would come along and just make all this stop.

It was starting to seep in what this might mean. What it *would* mean, in less time than the end of the school year. He would be dead. Gone. Anything he'd looked forward to would be cut short, anything he hoped for the future would be stopped by the fact that there would *be* no future.

Kevin wasn't sure how he felt about that. Sad, yes, because it was the kind of news you were supposed to feel sad about, and because he didn't want to die. Angry, because what he wanted didn't appear to matter when it came to this. Confused, because he wasn't sure why it should be him, when there were billions of other people in the world.

4

Compared to his mother, though, he was calm. She was shaking as she drove, and Kevin was so worried they might crash that he sighed with relief when they pulled onto the street where their house stood. It was one of the smallest houses on the block, old and patched with repairs.

"It will be all right," his mother said. She didn't sound as though she believed it. She took hold of Kevin's arm as they made their way into the house, but it felt more like Kevin was supporting her.

"It will be," Kevin replied, because he suspected that his mother needed to hear it even more than he did. It might have helped if it were true.

They went inside, and it felt almost wrong to do anything after that, as though doing normal things would have been a kind of betrayal, after the news Dr. Markham had given them. Kevin put a frozen pizza in the oven, while in the background, he could hear his mother sobbing on the sofa. He started to go to comfort her, but two things stopped him. The first was the thought that his mother probably wouldn't want him to. She had always been the strong one, the one looking after him even after his father left when he was just a baby.

The second was the vision.

He saw a landscape beneath a sky that seemed more purple than blue, the trees beneath oddly shaped, with fronds that reminded Kevin of the palm trees on the beaches, but trunks that twisted in ways palm trees never did. The sky looked as though the sun was setting, but the sun looked wrong somehow. Kevin couldn't work out how, because he hadn't spent time looking at the sun, but he knew it wasn't the same.

In one corner of his mind, numbers pulsed, over and over.

He was walking across a space covered with reddish sand now, and could feel his toes sinking into it. There were creatures there, small and lizard-like, that scuttled away when he came too close to them. He looked around...

...and the world dissolved into flames.

Kevin woke up on the kitchen floor, the oven's timer beeping to tell him the pizza was ready, the smell of burning food dragging him off the floor and over to the oven before his mother had to do it. He didn't want her to see him like this, didn't want to give her even more reasons to worry.

He took the pizza out, cut it into slices, and took them into the living room. His mother was on the couch, and although she'd stopped crying, her eyes were red. Kevin put the pizza down on the coffee table, sitting beside her and switching on the TV so they could at least *pretend* that things were normal.

"You shouldn't have to do this," his mother said, and Kevin didn't know if she meant the pizza or everything else. Right then, it didn't matter.

Still the numbers hung in his head: 23h 06m 29.283s, −05° 02′ 28.59.

CHAPTER TWO

Kevin wasn't sure he'd ever felt as tired as he did when he and his mother drove into the school's parking lot. The plan was to try to keep going as normal, but he felt as if he might fall asleep at any moment. *That* was a long way from normal.

That was probably because of the treatments. There had been a lot of treatments in the last few days. His mother had found more doctors, and each one had a different plan for trying to at least slow things down. That was what they said, every time, the words making it clear that even that would be something special, and that actually stopping things was something they couldn't hope for.

"Have a good day at school, honey," his mother said. There was something false about the brightness of it, a brittle edge that said just how hard she was having to try in order to produce a smile. Kevin knew she was making an effort for him, and he did his best, too.

"I'll try, Mom," he assured her, and he could hear that his own voice didn't sound natural either. It was as if both of them were playing roles because they were afraid of the truth underneath them. Kevin played his because he didn't want his mother crying again.

How many times had she cried now? How many days had it been since they'd been to see Dr. Markham the first time? Kevin had lost track. There had been a day or two off school sick, before it had become obvious that neither of them wanted that. Then there had been this: school interspersed with tests and attempts at therapies. There had been injections and blood tests, supplements because his mom had read online that they might help, and health food that was a long way from pizza.

"I just want things to be as normal as possible," his mother said. Neither of them mentioned that on a normal day, Kevin would have taken the bus to school, and they wouldn't have had to worry about what was normal or not.

Or that on a normal day, he wouldn't be hiding what was wrong with him, or feeling grateful that his closest friend went to a different school after the last time he and his mom had moved, so that she wouldn't have to see any of this. He hadn't called Luna in days now, and the messages were building up on his phone. Kevin ignored them, because he couldn't think of how to answer them.

7

Kevin could feel the eyes on him from the moment he went inside the school. The rumors had been going around now, even if no one knew for sure what was wrong with him. He could see a teacher ahead, Mr. Williams, and on a normal day Kevin would have been able to walk past him without even attracting a moment of attention. He wasn't one of the kids the teachers kept a close eye on because they were always doing something wrong. Now, the teacher stopped him, looking him up and down as if expecting signs that he might die at any moment.

"How are you feeling, Kevin?" he asked. "Are you all right?"

"I'm fine, Mr. Williams," Kevin assured him. It was easier to be fine than to try to explain the truth: how he was worried about his mother, and he was tired all the time from the attempts at treatment, how he was scared about what was going to happen next.

How the numbers were still going around in his head.

23h 06m 29.283s, −05° 02′ 28.59. They were there at the back of his mind, squatting like a toad that wouldn't move, impossible to forget, impossible to ignore, no matter how much Kevin tried to follow his mother's instructions to forget them.

"Well, just let us know if you need anything," the teacher said.

Kevin still wasn't sure how to reply to that. It was one of those kind things that people said that was kind of useless at the same time. The one thing he needed was the thing they couldn't give him: to undo all of this; for things to be normal again. Teachers knew a lot of things, but not that.

Still, he did his best to pretend to be normal all the way through his math class, and through most of history after that. Ms. Kapinski was telling them about some early European history, which Kevin wasn't sure was actually on any kind of test, but which had apparently been what she majored in at college, and so seemed to show up more than it should.

"Did you know that most of the Roman remains found in Northern Europe aren't actually Roman?" she said. Kevin generally liked Ms. Kapinski's classes, because she wasn't afraid to wander off the point and tell them about whatever fragments of the past entered her head. It was a reminder of just how much there had been in the world before any of them.

"So they're fake?" Francis de Longe asked. Ordinarily, Kevin might have been the one asking it, but he was enjoying the chance to be quiet, almost invisible.

"Not exactly," Ms. Kapinski said. "When I say they aren't Roman, I mean that they're remains left behind by people who had never been near what is now Italy. They were the local populations,

8

but as the Romans advanced, as they conquered, the local people realized that the best way to do well was to fit in with Roman ways. The way they dressed, the buildings they lived in, the language they spoke, they changed everything to make it clear which side they were on, and because it gave them a better chance of good positions in the new order." She smiled. "Then, when there were rebellions against Rome, one of the keys to being part of it was *not* using those symbols."

Kevin tried to imagine that: the same people in a place shifting who they were as the political tide changed, their whole being changing depending on who ruled. He thought it might be a bit like being in one of the popular crowds at school, trying to wear the right clothes and say the right things. Even so, it was hard to imagine, and not just because images of impossible landscapes continued to filter through at the back of his mind.

That was probably the only good thing about what was wrong with him: the symptoms were invisible. It was also the scary thing in a way. There was this thing killing him, and if people didn't know about it already, they would never find out. He could just sit there and no one would ever—

Kevin felt the vision coming, rising up through him like a kind of pressure building through his body. There was the rush of dizziness, the feeling of the world swimming away as he connected with something... else. He started to stand to ask if he could be excused, but by then, it was already too late. He felt his legs giving way and he collapsed.

He was looking at the same landscapes he remembered from before, the sky the wrong shade, the trees too twisted. He was watching the fire sweep through it, blinding and bright, seeming to come from everywhere at once. He'd seen all of that before. Now, though, there was a new element: a faint pulse that seemed to repeat at regular intervals, precise as a ticking clock.

Some part of Kevin knew a clock was what it had to be, just as he knew by instinct that it was counting down to something, not just marking the time. The pulses had the sense of getting subtly more intense, as if building up to some far-off crescendo. There was a word in a language he shouldn't have understood, but he *did* understand it.

"Wait."

Kevin wanted to ask what he was supposed to be waiting for, or how long, or why. He didn't, though, partly because he wasn't sure who he was supposed to ask, and partly because almost as suddenly as the moment had come, it passed, leaving Kevin rising

9

up from darkness to find himself lying on the floor of the classroom, Ms. Kapinski standing over him.

"Just lie still a moment, Kevin," she said. "I've sent for the school medic. Hal will be here in a minute."

Kevin sat up in spite of her instructions, because he'd come to know what this felt like by now.

"I'm fine," he assured her.

"I think we should let Hal be the judge of that."

Hal was a big, round former paramedic who served to make sure that the students of St. Brendan's School came through whatever medical emergencies they suffered. Sometimes, Kevin suspected that they did it because the thought of the medic's idea of care made them ignore the worst of injuries.

"I saw things," Kevin managed. "There was a planet, and a burning sun, and a kind of message... like a countdown."

In the movies, someone would have insisted on contacting somebody important. They would have recognized the message for what it was. There would have been meetings, and investigations. Someone would have *done* something about it. Outside of the movies, Kevin was just a thirteen-year-old boy, and Ms. Kapinski looked at him with a mixture of pity and mild bewilderment.

"Well, I'm sure it's nothing," she said. "It's probably normal to see all kinds of things if you're having this sort of... episode."

Around them, Kevin could hear the muttering from the others in his class. None of it made him feel better.

"...just fell down and started twitching..."

"...I heard he was sick, I hope you can't catch it..."

"...Kevin thinks he sees planets..."

The last one was the one that hurt. It made it sound as though he were going crazy. Kevin wasn't going crazy. At least, he didn't think he was.

Despite his best attempts to insist that he was fine, Kevin still had to go with Hal when the medic came. Had to sit in the medic's office while he shone lights in Kevin's eyes and asked questions about a condition so rare he obviously had no more clue than Kevin did what was going on.

"The principal wanted to see us once I was sure you were okay," he said. "Do you feel up to walking to his office, or should we ask him to come here?"

"I can walk," Kevin said. "I'm fine."

"If you say so," Hal said.

They made their way to the principal's office, and Kevin almost wasn't surprised to find that his mother was there. Of course they would have called her in for a medical emergency, of course she would be there if he collapsed, but that wasn't good, not when she was supposed to be at work.

"Kevin, are you okay?" his mother asked as soon as he arrived, turning to him and drawing him into a hug. "What happened?"

"I'm fine, Mom," Kevin said.

"Ms. McKenzie, I'm sure we wouldn't have called you in if it weren't serious," the principal said. "Kevin collapsed."

"I'm fine now," Kevin insisted.

It didn't seem to make any difference how many times he said that, though.

"Plus," the principal said, "it seems that he was pretty confused when he came around. He was talking about... well, other planets."

"Planets," Kevin's mother repeated. Her voice was flat when she said that.

"Ms. Kapinski says it disrupted her class quite a bit," the principal said. He sighed. "I'm wondering if maybe Kevin might be better off staying at home for a while."

He said it without looking at Kevin. There was a decision being made there, and although Kevin was at the heart of it, it was clear he didn't actually get a say.

"I don't want to miss school," Kevin said, looking at his mother. Surely she wouldn't want him to either.

"I think what we have to ask," the principal said, "is if, at this point, school is really the best thing Kevin can be doing with the time he has."

It was probably intended to be a kind way of putting it, but all it did was remind Kevin of what the doctor had said. Six months to live. It didn't seem like enough time for anything, let alone to have a life in. Six months' worth of seconds, each one ticking away in a steady beat that matched the countdown in his head.

"You're saying that there's no point to my son being in school because he'll be dead soon anyway?" his mother snapped back. "Is that what you're saying?"

"No, of course not," the principal said, hurriedly, raising his hands to placate her.

"That's what it sounds like you're saying," Kevin's mother said. "It sounds as though you're freaked out by my son's illness as much as the kids here."

"I'm saying that it's going to be hard to teach Kevin as this gets worse," the principal said. "We'll try, but... don't you want to make the most of the time you have left?"

He said that in a gentle tone that still managed to cut right to Kevin's heart. He was saying exactly what his mother had thought, just in gentler words. The worst part was that he was right. Kevin wasn't going to live long enough to go to college, or get a job, or do *anything* that he might need school to prepare for, so why bother being there.

"It's okay, Mom," he said, reaching out to touch her arm.

That seemed to be enough of an argument to convince his mother, and just that told Kevin how serious this all was. On any other occasion, he would have expected her to fight. Now it seemed that the fight had been sucked out of her.

They went out to the car in silence. Kevin looked back at the school. The thought hit him that he probably wouldn't be coming back. He hadn't even had a chance to say goodbye.

"I'm sorry they called you at work," Kevin said as they sat in the car. He could feel the tension there. His mom didn't turn the engine on, just sat.

"It's not that," she said. "It's just… it was getting easy to pretend that nothing was wrong." She sounded so sad then, so deeply hurt. Kevin had gotten used to the expression that meant she was trying to keep from crying. She wasn't succeeding.

"*Are* you okay, Kevin?" she asked, even though by then, he was the one holding onto her, as tightly as he could.

"I'm… I wish I didn't have to leave school," Kevin said. He'd never thought he would hear himself say that. He'd never thought that *anyone* would say that.

"We could go back in," his mother said. "I could tell the principal that I'm going to bring you back here tomorrow, and every day after that, until…"

She broke off.

"Until it gets too bad," Kevin said. He screwed his eyes tightly shut. "I think maybe it's already too bad, Mom."

He heard her hit the dashboard, the dull thud echoing around the car.

"I know," she said. "I know and I hate it. I hate this *disease* that's taking my little boy from me."

She cried again for a little while. In spite of his attempts to stay strong, Kevin did too. It seemed to take a long time before his mother was calm enough to say anything else.

"They said you saw… planets, Kevin?" she asked.

"I saw it," Kevin said. How could he explain what it was like? How real it was?

His mother looked over, and now Kevin had the sense of her struggling for the right words to say. Struggling to be comforting and firm and calm, all at the same time. "You get that this isn't real, right, honey? It's just... it's just the disease."

Kevin knew that he ought to understand it, but...

"It doesn't feel like that," Kevin said.

"I know it doesn't," his mother said. "And I hate that, because it's just a reminder that my little boy is slipping away. All of this, I wish I could make it go away."

Kevin didn't know what to say to that. He wished it would go away too.

"It *feels* real," Kevin said, even so.

His mother was quiet for a long time. When she finally spoke, her voice had the brittle, barely holding it together quality that only arrived since the diagnosis, but now had become far too familiar.

"Maybe... maybe it's time we took you to see that psychologist."

CHAPTER THREE

Dr. Linda Yalestrom's office wasn't anywhere near as medical looking as all the others Kevin had been in recently. It was her home, for one thing, in Berkeley, with the university close enough that it seemed to back up her credentials as surely as the certificates that were neatly framed on the wall.

The rest of it looked like the kind of home office Kevin expected from TV, with soft furnishings obviously relegated here after some previous move, a desk where clutter had crept in from the rest of the house, and a few potted plants that seemed to be biding their time, ready to take over.

Kevin found himself liking Dr. Yalestrom. She was a short, dark-haired woman in her fifties, whose clothes were brightly patterned and about as far from medical scrubs as it was possible to get. Kevin suspected that might be the point, if she spent a lot of time working with people who had received the worst news possible from doctors already.

"Come sit down, Kevin," she said with a smile, gesturing to a broad red couch that was well worn with years of people sitting on it. "Ms. McKenzie, why don't you give us a while? I want Kevin to feel that he can say anything he needs to say. My assistant will get you some coffee."

His mother nodded. "I'll be right outside."

Kevin went to sit on the couch, which turned out to be exactly as comfortable as it appeared. He looked around the room at pictures of fishing trips and vacations. It took him a while to realize something important.

"You're not in any of the photos in here," he said.

Dr. Yalestrom smiled at that. "Most of my clients never notice. The truth is, a lot of these are places I always wanted to go, or places I heard were interesting. I put them out because young men like you spend a lot of time staring around the room, doing anything but talk to me, and I figure you should at least have something to look at."

It seemed a bit like cheating to Kevin.

"If you work with people who are dying a lot," he said, "why do you have pictures of places you always wanted to go? Why put it off, when you've seen…"

"When I've seen how quickly it can all end?" Dr. Yalestrom asked, gently.

Kevin nodded.

"Maybe because of the wonderful human ability to know that and still procrastinate. Or maybe I *have* been to some of these places, and the reason I'm not in the pictures is just that I think one of me staring down at people is quite enough."

Kevin wasn't sure if those were good reasons or not. They didn't seem like enough, somehow.

"Where would you go, Kevin?" Dr. Yalestrom asked. "Where would you go if you could go anywhere?"

"I don't know," he replied.

"Well, think about it. You don't have to let me know right away."

Kevin shook his head. It was strange, talking to an adult this way. Generally, when you were thirteen, conversations came down to questions or instructions. With the possible exception of his mom, who was at work a lot of the time anyway, adults weren't really interested in what someone his age had to say.

"I don't know," he repeated. "I mean, I never really thought I'd get to go anywhere." He tried to think about places he might like to go, but it was hard to come up with anywhere, especially now that he only had a few months to do it. "I feel as though, wherever I think of, what's the point? I'll be dead pretty soon."

"What do you think the point is?" Dr. Yalestrom asked.

Kevin did his best to think of a reason. "I guess… because pretty soon is not the same thing as now?"

The psychologist nodded. "I think that's a good way to put it. So, is there anything that you would like to do in the pretty soon, Kevin?"

Kevin thought about it. "I guess… I guess I should tell Luna what's happening."

"And who's Luna?"

"She's my friend," Kevin said. "We don't go to the same school anymore, so she hasn't seen me collapse or anything, and I haven't called in a few days, but…"

"But you should tell her," Dr. Yalestrom said. "It isn't healthy to push away your friends when things get bad, Kevin. Not even to protect them."

Kevin swallowed back a denial, because it *was* kind of what he was doing. He didn't want to inflict this on Luna, didn't want to hurt her with the news of what was going to happen. It was part of the reason he hadn't called her in so long.

"What else?" Dr. Yalestrom said. "Let's try places again. If you could go anywhere, where would you go?"

Kevin tried to pick among all the places in the room, but the truth was that there was only one landscape that kept springing into his head, with colors no normal camera could capture.

"It would sound stupid," he said.

"There's nothing wrong with sounding stupid," Dr. Yalestrom assured him. "I'll tell you a secret. People often think that everyone else but them is special. They think that other people must be cleverer, or braver, or better, because only they can see the parts of themselves that aren't those things. They worry that everyone else says the right thing, and they sound stupid. It's not true though."

Even so, Kevin sat there for several seconds, examining the upholstery of the couch in detail. "I… I see places. One place. I guess it's the reason that I had to come here."

Dr. Yalestrom smiled. "You're here because an illness like yours can create a lot of odd effects, Kevin. I'm here to help you cope with them, without them dominating your life. Would you like to tell me more about the things you see?"

Again, Kevin made a detailed examination of the couch, learning its topography, picking at a tiny speck of lint sticking up from the rest. Dr. Yalestrom was silent while he did it; the kind of silence that felt as though it was sucking words up out of him, giving them a space to fall into.

"I see a place where nothing is quite the same as here. The colors are wrong, the animals and the plants are different," Kevin said. "I see it destroyed… at least, I think I do. There's fire and heat, a bright flash. There's a set of numbers. And there's something that feels like a countdown."

"Why does it feel like a countdown?" Dr. Yalestrom asked.

Kevin shrugged. "I'm not sure. Because the pulses are getting closer together, I guess?"

The psychologist nodded, then went over to her desk. She came back with paper and pencils.

"How are you at art?" she asked. "No, don't answer that. It doesn't matter if this is a great work of art or not. I just want you to try to draw what you see, so that I can get a sense of what it's like. Don't pay too much attention to it, just draw. Can you do that for me, Kevin?"

Kevin shrugged. "I'll try."

He took the pencils and paper, trying to bring the landscape that he'd seen to mind, trying to remember every detail of it. It was hard to do, because although the numbers stayed in his head, it felt as though he had to dive down deep into himself to pull up the images. They were below the surface, and to get at them, Kevin had to pull back into himself, concentrating on nothing else, letting the pencil flow over the paper almost automatically...

"Okay, Kevin," she said, taking the pad away before Kevin could get a good look at what he'd drawn. "Let's see what you've..."

He saw the look of shock that crossed her face, so brief that it almost wasn't there. It *was* there though, and Kevin had to wonder what it would take to shock someone who heard stories about people dying every day.

"What is it?" Kevin asked. "What did I draw?"

"You don't know?" Dr. Yalestrom asked.

"I was trying not to think too much," Kevin said. "Did I do something wrong?"

Dr. Yalestrom shook her head. "No, Kevin, you didn't do anything wrong."

She held out Kevin's drawing. "Would you like to take a look at what you produced? Perhaps it will help you to understand things."

She held it out folded, in just the tips of her fingers, as if she didn't want to touch it more than necessary. That made Kevin worry just a little. What could he have drawn that would make an adult react like that? He took it, unfolding it.

A drawing of a spaceship sat there, only "drawing" probably wasn't the right word for it. This was more like a blueprint, complete in every detail, which seemed impossible in the time Kevin had to draw. He'd never even seen this before, but here it was, on the page, looking giant and flat, like a city perched on a disk. There were smaller disks around it, like worker bees around a queen.

The detail meant that there was something neat, almost clinical, about the way it was drawn, but there was more to it than that. There was something about the geometry of it that was just... wrong, somehow, seeming to have depths and angles to it that shouldn't have been possible to capture just in a sketch like this.

"But this..." Kevin didn't know what to say. Didn't this prove what was happening? Did anyone think he could have just made something like this up?

Apparently, Dr. Yalestrom wasn't convinced though. She took back the picture, folding it carefully as though she didn't want to have to look at it. Kevin suspected that the strangeness of it was too much for her.

"I think it's important that we talk about the things you're seeing," she said. "Do you think those things are real?"

Kevin hesitated. "I'm... not sure. They *feel* real, but a lot of people now have told me that they can't be."

"It makes sense," Dr. Yalestrom said. "What you're feeling is very common."

"It is?" What he was experiencing didn't feel very common at all. "I thought that my illness was rare."

Dr. Yalestrom moved over to her desk, placing Kevin's drawing in a file. She picked up a tablet and started to make notes. "Is it important that other people shouldn't experience what you're experiencing, Kevin?"

"No, it's not that," Kevin said. "It was just that Dr. Markham said that this disease only affects a few people."

"That's true," Dr. Yalestrom agreed. "But I see a lot of people who experience hallucinations of some kind for other reasons."

"You think I'm going crazy," Kevin guessed. Everyone else seemed to. Even his mom, presumably, since she'd been the one to bring him here after he'd started talking about them. He didn't *feel* like he was going crazy, though.

"That's not a word I like to use here," Dr. Yalestrom said. "I think that often, the behavior that we label crazy is there for a good reason. It's just that often, those reasons only make sense to the person concerned. People will do things to protect themselves from situations that are too difficult to handle, which seem to be... unusual."

"You think that's what I'm doing with these visions?" Kevin asked. He shook his head. "They're real. I'm not making them up."

"Can I tell you what I think, Kevin? I think a part of you might be attached to these 'visions' because it's helping you to think that your illness might be happening for some kind of greater good. I think that maybe these 'visions' are actually you trying to make sense of your illness. The imagery in them... there's a strange place that isn't like the normal world. Could that represent the way things have changed?"

"I guess," Kevin said. He wasn't convinced. The things he'd seen weren't about some world where he didn't have his disease. They were about a place he didn't understand at all.

"Then you have the sense of impending doom with fire and light," Dr. Yalestrom said. "The sense of things coming to an end. You even have a countdown, complete with numbers."

The numbers weren't a part of the countdown; that was just the slow pulsing, growing faster bit by bit. Kevin suspected that he wasn't going to convince her of that now. When adults had decided what the truth of something was, he wasn't going to be able to change their minds.

"So what can I do?" Kevin asked. "If you think they aren't real, shouldn't I want to get rid of them?"

"Do *you* want to get rid of them?" Dr. Yalestrom asked.

Kevin thought about that. "I don't know. I think they might be important, but I didn't ask for them."

"The same way that you didn't ask to be diagnosed with a degenerative brain disease," Dr. Yalestrom said. "Maybe those two things are linked, Kevin."

Kevin had already been thinking that his visions were linked to the disease in some way. That maybe it had changed his brain enough to be receptive to the visions. He didn't think that was what the psychiatrist meant, though.

"So what can I do?" Kevin asked again.

"There are things you can do, not to make them go away, but at least to be able to cope."

"Such as?" Kevin asked. He had to admit to a moment of hope at the thought. He didn't want all of this going around and around in his head. He hadn't asked to be the one receiving messages that no one else understood, and that just made him look crazy when he spoke about them.

"You can try to find things to distract yourself from the hallucinations when they come," Dr. Yalestrom said. "You can try reminding yourself that it isn't real. If you're in doubt, find ways to check. Maybe ask someone else if they're seeing the same thing. Remember, it's okay to see whatever you see, but how you react to it is up to you."

Kevin guessed he could remember all that. Even so, it did nothing to quiet the faint pulse of the countdown, thrumming in the background, getting faster a little at a time.

"And I think you need to tell the people who don't know," Dr. Yalestrom said. "It isn't fair to them to keep them in the dark about this."

She was right.

And there was one person he needed to let know more than anyone else.

Luna.

CHAPTER FOUR

"So," Luna said, as she and Kevin made their way along one of the paths of the Lafayette Reservoir Recreation Area, dodging around the tourists and the families enjoying their day out, "why have you been avoiding me?"

Trust Luna to get straight to the point. It was one of the things Kevin liked about her. Not that he *liked* her liked her. People always seemed to assume that. They thought because she was pretty, and blonde, and probably cheerleader material if she didn't think all that was stupid, that of *course* they would be boyfriend and girlfriend. They just assumed that it was how the world worked.

They weren't together. Luna was his *best* friend. The person he spent the most time with, outside of school. Probably the one person in the world he could talk to about absolutely anything.

Except, it turned out, this.

"I haven't been…" Kevin trailed off in the face of Luna's stare. She was good at stares. Kevin suspected that she probably practiced. He'd seen everyone from bullies to rude store owners back down rather than have her stare at them any longer. Faced with that stare, it was impossible to lie to her. "All right, I have, but it's hard, Luna. I have something… well, something I don't know how to tell you."

"Oh, don't be stupid," Luna said. She found an abandoned soda can and kicked it down the path, flicking it from foot to foot with the kind of skill that came from doing it far too often. "I mean, how bad can it be? Are you moving away? Are you changing schools again?"

Maybe she caught something in his expression, because she fell silent for a few seconds. There was something fragile about that silence, as if both of them were tiptoeing to avoid breaking it. Even so, they had to. They couldn't just walk like this forever.

"Something bad then?" she said, sending the can into a trash container with a final flick of her foot.

Kevin nodded. Bad was one word for it.

"How bad?"

"Bad," he said. "The reservoir?"

The reservoir was the place they both went when they wanted to sit down and talk about things. They'd talked about Billy Hames liking Luna when they were nine, and about Kevin's cat, Tiger,

20

dying when they were ten. None of it seemed like a good preparation for this. He wasn't a cat.

They made their way down to the edge of the water, looking out at the trees on the far side, the people with their canoes and their paddle boats on the reservoir. Compared to some of the places they went, this was nice. People assumed Kevin was the kid from the wrong side of town leading Luna astray, but she was the one with the knack for squeezing past fences and clambering up derelict buildings, leaving Kevin to follow if he could. Here, there was none of that, just the water and the trees.

"What is it?" Luna asked. She kicked off her shoes and dangled her feet in the water. Kevin didn't feel like doing the same. Right then, he wanted to run, to hide. Anything to keep from telling her the truth. It felt as though, the longer he could keep from telling Luna, the longer it wasn't really real.

"Kevin?" Luna said. "You're worrying me now. Look, if you don't tell me what it is, then I'm going to call your mom and find out that way."

"No, don't do that," Kevin said quickly. "I'm not sure... Mom isn't handling this well."

Luna was looking more worried by the moment. "What's wrong? Is she sick? Are *you* sick?"

Kevin nodded at the last one. "I'm sick," he said. He put his hand on Luna's shoulder. "I have something called leukodystrophy. I'm dying, Luna."

He knew he'd said it too quickly. Something like that, there should be a whole big explanation, a proper build-up, but honestly, that was the part of it that mattered.

She stared at him, shaking her head in obvious disbelief. "No, you can't be, that's..."

She hugged him then, tight enough that Kevin could barely breathe.

"Tell me it's a joke. Tell me it's not real."

"I wish it weren't," Kevin said. He wished that more than anything right then.

Luna pulled back, and Kevin could see her screwing her features tight with the effort of not crying. Normally, Luna was good at not crying about things. Now, though, he could see it taking everything she had.

"This... how long?" she asked.

"They said maybe six months," Kevin said.

21

"And that was *days* ago, so it's less now," Luna shot back. "And you've been having to cope with it on your own, and…" She faded into silence as the sheer enormity of it obviously hit her.

Kevin could see her looking out at the people on the reservoir, watching them with their small boats and their quick forays into the water. They seemed so happy there. She stared at them as if they were the part she couldn't believe, not the illness.

"It doesn't seem fair," she said. "All these people, just going on as if the world is the same, going about having fun when you're *dying*."

Kevin smiled sadly. "What are we supposed to do? Tell them all to stop having fun?"

He realized the danger in saying that slightly too late as Luna leapt to her feet, cupped her hands to her mouth, and yelled at the top of her voice.

"Hey, all of you, you have to stop! My friend is dying, and I demand that you stop having fun at once!"

A couple of people looked around, but no one stopped. Kevin suspected that hadn't been the point. Luna stood there for several seconds, and this time, he was the one to hug her, holding her while she cried. That was enough of a rarity that the sheer shock value of it held Kevin there. Luna shouting at people, behaving in ways that they would never expect from someone like her, was normal. Luna breaking down wasn't.

"Feel better?" he asked after a while.

She shook her head. "Not really. What about you?"

"Well, it's nice to know that there's someone who would try to stop the world for me," he said. "You know the worst part?"

Luna managed another smile. "Not being able to spell what's killing you?"

Kevin could only return that smile. Trust Luna to know that he needed her to be her usual self, making fun of him.

"I can, I practiced. The worst part is that all this means no one believes me when I tell them that I've been seeing things. They think it's all just the illness."

Luna cocked her head to one side. "What kind of things?"

Kevin explained to her about the strange landscapes he'd been seeing, the fire wiping it clean, the sensation of a countdown.

"That…" Luna began when he was finished. She didn't seem to know how to end though.

"I know, it's crazy, I'm crazy," Kevin said. Even Luna didn't believe him.

"You didn't let me finish," Luna said, drawing in a breath. "That... is *so* cool."

"Cool?" Kevin repeated. It hadn't been the response he expected, even from her. "Everyone else thinks I'm going crazy, or my brain is melting, or something."

"Everyone else is stupid," Luna declared, although, to be fair, that seemed to be her default setting for life. To her, everyone was stupid until proven otherwise.

"So you believe me?" Kevin said. Even he wasn't completely sure anymore, after everything people had said to him.

Luna held onto his shoulders, looking him squarely in the eyes. With another girl, Kevin might have thought she was about to kiss him. Not with Luna, though.

"If you tell me that these visions are real, then they're real. I believe you. And being able to see alien worlds is definitely cool."

Kevin's eyes widened a little at that. "What makes you think that it's an alien world?"

Luna stepped back with a shrug. "What else is it going to be?"

When she asked that, Kevin got the feeling that she was every bit as stunned by all this as he was. She just did a better job of hiding it.

"Maybe..." she guessed, "...maybe all this has changed your brain, so that it has a direct line to this alien place?"

If Luna ever acquired a superpower, it would probably be the ability to leap tall conclusions in a single bound. Kevin liked that about her, especially when it meant that she was the one person who might believe him, but even so, it felt like a lot to decide, so quickly.

"You know how crazy that sounds, right?" he said.

"No crazier than the idea that the world is just going to snatch my friend away for no good reason," Luna shot back, her fists clenched in a way that suggested she would happily fight it over the issue. Or maybe just clenched with the effort of not crying again. Luna tended to get angry, or make jokes, or do crazy things rather than be upset. Right then, Kevin couldn't blame her.

He watched her coming down from whatever nearly crying space she was in, winding down from it piece by piece and forcing a smile into the space instead.

"So, terrible disease, cool visions of alien worlds... is there anything else you aren't telling me?"

"Just the numbers," Kevin said.

Luna looked at him with obvious annoyance. "You get that you weren't supposed to say yes there?"

"I wanted to tell you everything," Kevin said, although he guessed it was probably a bit late now. "Sorry."

"Okay," Luna said. Again, Kevin had the sense of her working to process it all. "Numbers?"

"I see them too," Kevin said. He repeated them from memory. "23h 06m 29.283s, −05° 02′ 28.59."

"Okay," Luna said. She pursed her lips. "I wonder what they mean."

That they might not mean anything seemed not to occur to her. Kevin loved that about her.

She had her phone out. "It's not right for a license plate, and it would be weird for a password. What else?"

Kevin hadn't thought about it, at least not with the kind of directness that Luna seemed to be applying to the problem.

"Maybe like an item number, a serial number?" Kevin suggested.

"But there are hours and minutes there," Luna said. She seemed utterly caught up in the problem of what it might mean. "What else?"

"Maybe like a delivery time and a location?" Kevin suggested. "Those second parts sound like they might be coordinates."

"It's not quite right for a map reference," Luna said. "Maybe if I just Google it… oh, cool."

"What?" Kevin asked. One look at Luna's face said that they'd hit the jackpot.

"When you type that string of numbers into a search engine, you only get results about one thing," Luna said. She made it sound so certain like that. She turned her phone to show him, the pages set out in a neat row. "The Trappist 1 star system."

Kevin could feel his excitement building. More than that, he could feel his *hope* building. Hope that this might really mean something, and that it *wasn't* just his illness, no matter what anyone said. Hope that it might actually be real.

"Why would I see those numbers, though?" he asked.

"Maybe because the Trappist system is supposed to be one of the ones that have a chance of harboring life?" Luna said. "From what it says here, there are several planets there in what we think is a habitable zone."

She said it as if it were the most obvious thing in the world. The idea of planets that might have life seemed like too much to be a coincidence when Kevin had *seen* that life. Or seen some strange life, at least.

"You need to talk to someone about this," Luna declared. "You're... like, the first proof of extraterrestrial contact, or something. Who were those people looking for aliens, the scientists? I saw a thing about them on TV."

"SETI?" Kevin said.

"Those are the ones," Luna said. "Aren't they based in San Francisco, or San Jose, or something?"

Kevin hadn't known that, but the more he thought about it, the more the idea tugged at him.

"You have to go, Kevin," Luna said. "You have to at least talk to them."

***

"No," his mother said, setting her coffee down so firmly it spilled. "No, Kevin, absolutely not!"

"But Mom—"

"I'm not driving you to San Francisco so that you can bother a bunch of nutjobs," his mother said.

Kevin held out his phone, showing the information about SETI on it. "They aren't crazy," he said. "They're scientists."

"Scientists can be crazy too," his mother said. "And this whole idea... Kevin, can't you just accept that you're seeing things that aren't there?"

That was the problem; it would be all too easy to accept it. It would be easy to tell himself that this wasn't real, but there was something nagging away at the back of his brain that said it would be a really bad idea if he did. The countdown was still going, and Kevin suspected that he needed to talk to someone who would believe him before it reached its end.

"Mom, the numbers I told you I was seeing... they turned out to be the location for a star system."

"There are so many stars out there that I'm sure any random string of numbers would connect to one of them," his mother said. "It would be the same as the mass of the star or... or, I don't know enough about stars to know what else, but it would be something."

"I don't mean that," Kevin said. "I mean it was exactly the same. Luna put the numbers in and the Trappist 1 system was the first thing to come out. The *only* thing to come out."

"I should have known that Luna would be involved," his mother said with a sigh. "I love that girl, but she has too much imagination for her own good."

"Please, Mom," Kevin said. "This is real."

His mother reached out to put her hands on his shoulders. When had she started having to reach up to do that? "It's not, Kevin. Dr. Yalestrom said that you were having trouble accepting all this. You have to understand what's going on, and I have to help you to accept it."

"I know I'm dying, Mom," Kevin said. He shouldn't have put it like that, because he could see the tears rising in his mother's eyes.

"Do you? Because this—"

"I'll find a way to get there," Kevin promised. "I'll take a bus if I have to. I'll take a train into the city and walk. I have to at least *talk* to them."

"And get laughed at?" His mother pulled away, not looking at him. "You know that's what will happen, right, Kevin? I'm trying to protect you."

"I know you are," Kevin said. "And I know that they'll probably laugh at me, but I have to at least try, Mom. I have the feeling that this is really important."

He wanted to say more, but he wasn't sure that more would help right then. His mother was quiet in the way that said she was thinking, and right then, that was the best that Kevin could hope for. She kept thinking, her hand drumming on the kitchen counter, marking time as she made up her mind.

Kevin heard his mother's sigh.

"All right," she said. "I'll do it. I'll take you, but only because I suspect that, if I don't, I'll be getting a call from the police to tell me that my son has collapsed on a bus somewhere."

"Thanks, Mom," Kevin said, moving forward to hug her.

He knew she didn't really believe him, but in a way, that made the show of love even more impressive.

CHAPTER FIVE

It took around an hour to drive from Walnut Creek down to the SETI Institute in Mountain View, but to Kevin, it felt like a lifetime. It wasn't just that traffic into the city crawled its way through road closures; every moment was something wasted when he could be there, could be finding out what was going on with him. They would know, he was certain of it.

"Try not to get too excited," his mother warned him, for what seemed like the twentieth time. Kevin knew she was just trying to protect him, but even so, he didn't want his excitement dampened. He was sure that this would be the place where he found out what was going on. They were scientists who studied aliens. Surely they would know everything?

When they got there, though, the institute wasn't what he was expecting. 189 Bernardo Avenue looked more like an art gallery or a part of a university than the kind of ultra-high-tech buildings Kevin's imagination had conjured up. He'd been expecting buildings that looked as though they might be from outer space, but instead, they looked a little like expensive versions of the kind of buildings his school had.

They drove up and parked in front of the buildings. Kevin took a breath. This was it. They walked into a lobby, where a woman smiled over at them, managing to turn that into a question even before she spoke.

"Hello, are you sure that you're in the right place?"

"I need to talk to someone about alien signals," Kevin said, before his mother could try to explain.

"I'm sorry," the woman said. "We don't really have public tours."

Kevin shook his head. He knew he needed to get her to understand. "I'm not here for a tour," he said. "I think... I think I'm receiving some kind of alien signal."

The woman didn't look at him with the kind of shock and disbelief that most other people might have, or even with the surprise his mother had at him coming out with it like that. This was more a look of resignation, as if she had to put up with this kind of thing more often than she would like.

"I see," she said. "Unfortunately, we're not in a position to talk to people who walk in off the street. If you want to send a message

27

to us through our contact email, we'd be happy to consider it, but for the moment…"

"Come on, Kevin," his mother said. "We tried."

To his own surprise as much as anyone's. Kevin shook his head. "No, I'm not going."

"Kevin, you have to," his mother said.

Kevin sat down, right there in the middle of the lobby. The carpet wasn't very comfortable, but he didn't care. "I'm not going anywhere until I speak to someone about this."

"Wait, you can't do that," the receptionist said.

"I'm not going anywhere," Kevin said.

"Kevin…" his mother began.

Kevin shook his head. He knew it was childish, but the way he saw it, he was thirteen, and he was allowed. Besides, this was important. If he walked out and left now, this was over. He couldn't let it be over.

"Get up, or I'll have to call security," the receptionist said. She walked to him and took hold of Kevin's arm in a firm grip.

Instantly, Kevin's mother switched her attention from him to the receptionist, her eyes narrowing.

"Take your hands off my son, right now."

"Then make your son get up and leave before I have to get the police involved." The receptionist let go anyway, although that might have had something to do with the look his mother gave her. Kevin had the feeling that, now that there was one way she *could* protect her son, his mother was going to do it, whatever it took.

"Don't you threaten us with the police. Kevin isn't doing anyone any harm."

"You think we don't get crazies here on a regular basis?"

"Kevin is *not* crazy!" his mother shouted, at a volume she normally reserved for when Kevin had done something *really* wrong.

The next couple of minutes featured more arguing than Kevin was happy with. His mother shouted at him to get up. The receptionist shouted that she would call security. They shouted at each other, as Kevin's mother decided that she didn't want anyone threatening her son with security, and the woman seemed to assume that his mother would be able to move Kevin. Kevin sat through it all with surprising serenity.

It lulled him down, and in those depths, he saw something…

The cold darkness of space stood around him, stars flickering, with the Earth looking so different from above that it almost took Kevin's breath away. There was a silvery object floating there in

28

space, just one of so many others hanging in orbit. The words *Pioneer 11* were stenciled on the side…

Then he was lying on the SETI Institute's floor, his mother helping him up, along with the receptionist.

"Is he okay?" the receptionist asked. "Do you need me to call an ambulance?"

"No, I'm fine," Kevin insisted.

His mother shook her head. "We know what's wrong. My son is dying. All of this… I thought it would help him to come to terms with the fact that what he was seeing wasn't real, that it was the illness."

Put like that, it felt like a betrayal, as if Kevin's mother had been planning for his dreams to be crushed all along.

"I understand," the receptionist said. "Okay, let's get you up, Kevin. Can I get you both anything?"

"I just want to talk to someone," Kevin said.

The receptionist bit her lip, then nodded. "Okay, I'll see what I can do."

Just like that, her whole attitude seemed to have changed.

"Wait here. Take a seat. I'll go and see if there's anyone around who can at least talk to you, maybe show you around. Although there really isn't much to see."

Kevin sat down with his mother. He wanted to tell her about everything he'd just seen, but he could see from her face that it would only hurt her. He waited in silence instead.

Finally, a woman came out. She was in her early fifties, dressed in a dark suit that suggested she had the kind of meetings where more casual clothes wouldn't work. There was something about her that said she was an academic—maybe something in the curiosity with which she looked at Kevin. She offered his mother her hand, and then Kevin.

"Hello, Kevin," she said. "I'm Dr. Elise Levin. I'm the director here at the institute."

"You're in charge?" Kevin asked, hope rising in him. "Of all the alien stuff?"

She smiled with amusement. "I think that's putting it a bit strongly. A lot of the search for extraterrestrial life happens elsewhere. NASA provides data, some universities get involved, and we often borrow time on other people's telescopes where we can. But yes, I'm in charge of this institute and the things that go on here."

"Then I need to tell you," Kevin said. He was speaking quicker than he wanted to, trying to get the words out before this adult had time to disbelieve him. "There's something happening. I know how strange it sounds, but I've been seeing things, there's a kind of countdown…"

How could he explain the countdown? It wasn't like numbers, there wasn't an obvious point he could say marked its end. There was just a faint pulse that came with the signal in his brain, getting steadily, almost imperceptibly faster as it worked its way toward something that Kevin couldn't guess at.

"Why don't you tell me about it while we take a look around?" Dr. Levin suggested. "I'll show you some of what we do here."

She led Kevin and his mother through the institute's corridors, and to be honest, Kevin had thought that it would be more exciting. He'd thought it would look less like an office block.

"I thought there would be big telescopes here, or labs full of equipment for testing things from space," Kevin said.

Dr. Levin shrugged. "We have some laboratories, and we do test materials occasionally, but we don't have any telescopes. We are working with Berkeley to build a dedicated radio telescope array though."

"Then how do you look for aliens?" Kevin's mother said. It seemed that she was as surprised by the lack of giant telescopes and listening equipment as Kevin was.

"We work with other people," Dr. Levin said. "We ask for, or hire, time on telescopes and sensor arrays. We work with data from NASA. We put in suggestions to them about places they might want to look, or kinds of data they might want to try to gather. I'm sorry, I know it isn't as exciting as people sometimes think. Here, come with me."

She led the way to an office that at least looked a bit more interesting than some of the other spaces. It held a couple of computers, a lot of posters relating to the solar system, a few magazines that had mentioned SETI's work, and some furniture that looked as though it had been especially designed to be ergonomic, stylish, and about as comfortable as a brick.

"Let me show you some of the things we've been working on," Dr. Levin said, calling up images of large telescope arrays in the process of being built. "We're looking at developing radio telescope arrays that might be powerful enough to pick up ambient radio frequencies rather than just waiting for someone to target us with a signal."

"But I think someone *is* signaling to us," Kevin said. He needed to get her to understand.

Dr. Levin paused. "I was going to ask if you're referring to the theory that what some people think are high-frequency radio bursts from a pulsar might be intelligible signals, but you're not, are you?"

"I've been seeing things," Kevin said. He tried to explain about the visions. He told her about the landscape he'd seen, and about the countdown.

"I see," Dr. Levin said. "But I have to ask something, Kevin. You understand that SETI is about exploring this issue with science, seeking real proof? It's the only way that we can do this and know that anything we find is real. So, I have to ask you, Kevin, how do you know what you're seeing is real?"

Kevin had already managed to answer that with Luna. "I saw some numbers. When I looked them up, it turned out that they were the location for something called the Trappist 1 system."

"One of the more promising candidates for alien life," Dr. Levin said. "Even so, Kevin, do you understand my problem now? You say you saw these numbers, and I believe you, but maybe you saw them because you'd read them somewhere. I can't redirect SETI's resources based on that, and in any case, I'm not sure what else we could do when it comes to the Trappist 1 system. For something like that, I would need something new. Something you couldn't have gotten another way."

Kevin could tell that she was trying to let him down as gently as possible, but even so, it hurt. How could he provide them with that? Then he thought about what he'd seen in the lobby. He had to have seen that for a reason, didn't he?

"I think…" He wasn't sure whether to say it or not, but he knew he had to. "I think you're going to get a signal from something called Pioneer 11."

Dr. Levin looked at him for a couple of seconds. "I'm sorry, Kevin, but that doesn't seem very likely."

Kevin saw his mother frown. "What's Pioneer 11?"

"It's one of the deep space probes NASA has sent out," Dr. Levin explained. "It flew through our solar system, sending back data, and had enough velocity to send it out past the limits of the solar system. Unfortunately, the last contact that we had with it was in 1995, so I really don't think that—"

She stopped as her phone started to ring, taking it out as if to ignore the call. Kevin saw the moment when she stopped and stared.

"I'm sorry, I have to take this," she said. "Yes, hello, what is it? Can it wait a moment, I'm in the middle of… okay, if it's that urgent. A signal? You're calling me because NASA has data coming in? But NASA always has…" She paused again, looking over at Kevin, the disbelief obvious on her face. Even so, she said it. "Can I take a guess?" she said into the phone. "You've just had a signal of some kind from Pioneer 11? You have? No, I can't tell you. I'm not sure you would believe me if I did."

She put the phone down, staring at Kevin as if seeing him for the first time in that moment.

"How did you do that?" she asked.

Kevin shrugged. "I saw it when I was waiting in the lobby."

"You saw it? The same way that you 'saw' this alien landscape?" Dr. Levin stared at him, and Kevin had the sense she was trying to work something out. Probably trying to work out any way he could have cheated this, or made it happen.

It was almost a minute before she came to a decision.

"I think," Dr. Levin said, in the careful tones of someone trying to make sure she hadn't gone crazy, "that you had better come with me."

CHAPTER SIX

Kevin and his mother followed Dr. Levin from SETI's facility to a car that seemed far too small to belong to someone in her position.

"It's very environmentally friendly," she said, in a tone that suggested she had faced that question a lot. "Come on, it will be easier if I drive you both over. They're quite strict about security."

"Who is?" Kevin's mother asked.

"NASA."

Kevin's breath caught at that. They were going to talk to NASA? When it came to aliens, that was even better than SETI.

The drive across Mountain View was only a short one, a few minutes at most. Even so, it was long enough for Kevin to stare out the windows at the high-tech companies spread around the area, obviously drawn there by NASA and Berkeley, the presence of so many clever people in one place pulling them in.

"We're really going to NASA?" Kevin said. He couldn't quite believe it, which made no sense, given all the things he'd had to believe in the last few days.

The NASA campus was everything that the SETI building hadn't been. It was large, spread across several buildings and set in a space that managed to have views of both the surrounding hills and the bay. There was a visitors center that was essentially a tent built on a scale that seemed hard to believe, bright white and painted with the NASA logo. They drove past that, though, to a space that was closed off to the public, behind a chain-link fence and a barrier where Dr. Levin had to show ID to get them in.

"I'm expected," she said.

"And who are they, ma'am?" the guard asked.

"This is Kevin McKenzie and his mother," Dr. Levin said. "They're with me."

"They're not on the—"

"They're with me," Dr. Levin said again, and for the first time, Kevin had a sense of the kind of toughness involved in her position. The guard hesitated for a moment, then produced a couple of visitors' passes, which Dr. Levin handed over to them. Kevin hung his around his neck, and it felt like a trophy, a talisman. With this, he could go where he needed. With this, people actually *believed* him.

"We'll need to go into the research areas," Dr. Levin said. "Please be careful not to touch anything, because some of the experiments are delicate."

She led the way inside a building that appeared to be composed mostly of delicate curves of steel and glass. This was the kind of place Kevin had been expecting when they came down to Mountain View. This was what a place that looked out into space should be. There were laboratories to either side, with the kind of advanced equipment in them that suggested they could test almost anything space threw their way. There were lasers and computers, benches and devices that looked designed for chemistry. There were workshops full of welding equipment and parts that might have been for cars, but that Kevin wanted to believe were for vehicles for use on other planets.

Dr. Levin asked around as they went, apparently trying to find out where everyone was who was connected with the news about Pioneer 11's message. Whenever they passed someone, she stopped them, and it seemed to Kevin that she knew everyone there. SETI might be separate from all of this, the way she said it was, but it was obvious that Dr. Levin spent a lot of time here.

"Hey, Marvin, where is everybody?" she asked a bearded man in a checked shirt.

"They're mostly gathered in the center for supercomputer research," he said. "Something like this, they want to see what the pits will come up with."

"The pits?" Kevin asked.

Dr. Levin smiled. "You'll see."

"Who are they?" the bearded man asked.

"What would you say if I told you that Kevin here can see aliens?" Dr. Levin asked.

Marvin laughed. "You can try to play up to the crazy alien hunter reputation all you want, Elise. You're as skeptical as the rest of us."

"Maybe not about this," Dr. Levin said. She looked back at Kevin and his mother. "This way."

She led the way to another part of the building, and now Kevin had the sense of extra security, with ID scanners and cameras at almost every turn. More than that, it was probably the *cleanest* place he had ever been. Much cleaner than, for example, his bedroom. It seemed that not a speck of dust was allowed to intrude on it without permission, let alone the piles of old clothes that filled his space until his mom told him to tidy it.

The labs were mostly empty at the moment, and empty in ways that suggested they'd been left in a hurry because something more exciting was happening. It was easy to see where they had gone. People crowded in the corridors as the three of them got closer to their destination, exchanging gossip that Kevin only caught fragments of.

"There's a signal, an actual *signal*."

"After all this time."

"It's not just telemetry data, or even scans. There's something… else."

"We're here," Dr. Levin said, as they arrived at a room where the door had been left open, obviously to allow for the crowd of people trying to cram inside. "Let us through, please. We need to talk to Sam."

"Here" turned out to be a large room, filled with blinking lights below and surrounded by walkways that made it seem a bit like a theater where the actors were all computers. Kevin recognized them as computers even though they were nothing like the small, barely working laptop his mother had bought for him to do schoolwork on. These were devices the size of coffee tables, cars, rooms, all matte black and glittering with lights. The people standing or sitting close to them had on suits like the ones forensics people wore on TV shows.

"Impressed?" Dr. Levin asked.

Kevin could only nod. He didn't have the words for a place like this. It was… incredible.

"What is this place?" his mother asked, and Kevin didn't know if it was a good or bad thing that even his mother didn't understand it.

"It's where NASA does its supercomputer research," Dr. Levin explained. "Work on AI, quantum computing, more advanced superconductors. It's also the equipment they use to work on… complex issues. Come on, we need to talk to Sam."

She led the way through the crowd and Kevin followed, trying to be quick enough to move into the gaps she created before they closed again. He hurried along in her wake until they came to a tall, slightly stooped man standing by one of the computers. Unlike the others, he wasn't wearing a clean suit. His long, bony fingers seemed to be tying themselves in knots as he typed.

"Professor Brewster," Dr. Levin said.

"Dr. Levin, I'm glad you could… wait, you've brought visitors. This really isn't the moment for sightseeing, Elise."

If Dr. Levin was annoyed by that, she didn't show it. "David, this is Kevin McKenzie, and his mother. They're not here to sightsee. I think Kevin might prove helpful with this. We need to see Sam."

Professor Brewster waved a hand at the machine in front of them. It was even taller than he was, with pipes running up the side that were so cold they gave off steam into the air. It was only when Kevin saw the sign on the side, "*Signals Analysis Machine,*" that he realized Sam wasn't a person's name, but an acronym.

"You want to let a child play with a multimillion-dollar piece of engineering?" Professor Brewster asked. "I mean, he's what? Ten?"

"I'm thirteen," Kevin said. The difference might not be much to someone Professor Brewster's age, but to him, it was a fourth of his life. It was *more* life than he had remaining. Put like that, three years was a huge amount.

"Well, I'm forty-three, I have a doctorate from Princeton, a building full of often frankly impossible geniuses who should *be doing their jobs*"—he looked around the room pointedly, but no one moved—"and now, apparently a thirteen-year-old who wants to play with my supercomputer just as it is about to get to work on a signal from a probe we thought long dead."

He seemed like a man who didn't like stress much. Kevin guessed that was probably a disadvantage in his job.

"Kevin's here *because* of the signal," Dr. Levin said. "He… well, he predicted that it would occur."

"Impossible," Professor Brewster said. "Elise, you know I have always respected your efforts to keep SETI research in the realm of serious science, but this seems to run in completely the opposite direction. It's obviously a trick."

Dr. Levin sighed. "I know what I saw, David. He told me that there would be something happening with Pioneer 11, and then we got the signal. Will you at least play it for us?"

"Oh, very well," Professor Brewster said. He gestured to one of the scientists working around the supercomputer. "Play it so that we can get on with our work."

The scientist nodded and tapped a control interface a few times. Data flashed up on a screen in string after string of numbers, but Kevin was more interested in the audio signal that came with it. It was a strange mechanical chattering that sounded nothing like language, more like the kind of interference that might come from a computer going wrong.

Even so, he understood it. He just didn't know how.

"You need to adjust one of your radio telescopes," Kevin said, the knowledge just sitting in his mind. There were numbers too. Two sets of them, one marginally different from the other. "I think... the first seems wrong somehow, and the second is what it should be."

"What?" Professor Brewster and Dr. Levin asked almost simultaneously, although with very different expressions. Dr. Levin looked amazed. Professor Brewster mostly looked irritated.

"It's what it means," Kevin said. He shrugged. "I mean, I guess. I don't know how I know it."

"You *don't* know it," Professor Brewster insisted. "If there's any meaning in there at all, which frankly isn't likely, it will take SAM hours to decode it, if it's possible at all.

"I just told you what it means," Kevin insisted. "I can... it just makes sense to me."

"You should listen to him, David," Dr. Levin said. "At least search for the numbers, see if they mean anything. Can you write them down, Kevin?"

She held out a piece of paper and a pen, and Kevin noted them as clearly as he could. He held it out to Professor Brewster, who took it with bad grace.

"We have better things to do than this, Elise," he said. "Right, that's enough. Out. We have work to do here."

He shooed them away, and Dr. Levin didn't seem inclined to argue. Instead, she took Kevin and his mother out into the corridors of the research facility again.

"Come on," she said. "David might be too busy to actually use that gigantic brain of his, but there are plenty of people here who owe me favors."

"What kind of favors?" Kevin's mother asked.

Dr. Levin looked back at Kevin. "The kind where we find out exactly how Kevin is managing to receive and decode signals from outer space."

***

"You need to hold still, Kevin," said an overweight researcher wearing a Hawaiian shirt under his lab coat. He just went by "Phil" even though the nameplate on his door declared that he had at least as many PhDs as anyone else. He seemed to be a friend of Dr. Levin's, although that might have had something to do with the foot-long sandwich she picked up from the canteen before going to visit him. "It won't produce a clear image if you move."

Kevin did his best, lying still in the cramped interior of an MRI machine. It made him feel like a torpedo about to be launched into the ocean, and the confined space was only made worse by a regular dull thudding, which sounded as though someone was hammering on the outside of it while he lay there. His experiences in the hospital told him that was probably normal, and not a sign that the whole thing was about to collapse. Even so, it was hard to hold still for as long as it took for the thing to scan him.

"Almost there," Phil called. "Just hold your breath for a moment. And relax."

Kevin wished he could relax. The last couple of hours had been busy ones. There had been scientists, and labs, and tests. Lots of tests. There were cognitive tests and imaging scans, things like X-rays and word association tests while Kevin found various kinds of devices pointed at him, designed to pump different kinds of signals toward his body.

Eventually, even Phil seemed to be getting tired of shooting rays at Kevin.

"Okay, you can come out."

He helped Kevin from the machine, then led the way over to where Dr. Levin and Kevin's mother were waiting. The researcher shook his head as he pointed to the screen, and a series of black-and-white images that Kevin guessed must be of the inside of his brain. If so, brains looked weirder than he'd thought.

"I'm sorry, Elise, but there's no sign of anything different about him that wouldn't be explained by his illness," he said.

"Keep looking," Dr. Levin said.

"How, exactly?" he asked. "I'm telling you, I've used almost every test it's possible to do on a human being—fMRI, CAT scan, psych battery, you name it. I've fired so many different frequencies at Kevin here that it's a wonder he isn't picking up the local radio. Short of subjecting him to radioactive isotopes or actually dissecting him—"

"No," Kevin's mother said, firmly. Kevin didn't like that idea either.

Phil shook his head. "There's just nothing else there to find."

Kevin could hear the man's disappointment. Unlike Professor Brewster, he obviously *liked* the idea of someone being able to hear alien signals. That disappointment mirrored his own. He'd been sure that these people, with all their brains and their laboratories, would be able to find out what was happening, but it looked—

A man burst into the room, and it took Kevin a moment to recognize the gangly frame of Professor Brewster. He looked, if anything, even more agitated than he had when he'd been throwing them out of the supercomputer pit. He was holding a tablet, gripping it so tightly that Kevin suspected he might crack it.

"David, if this is about the use of resources…" Dr. Levin began.

The tall scientist looked over at her as if trying to work out what she was talking about, then shook his head. "Not that. I just want to know how you did it. How did you *know*?"

"Know what?" Kevin asked.

"Don't play dumb," the scientist said. He held out the tablet for them to look at. "One of our people ran those numbers you gave us through our systems. It turns out that they were the current settings for one of our radio telescopes, just as you said. No one who wasn't working at the observatory could know that. So how did you know?"

"Know what?" Kevin asked.

"Know what would happen when we changed it!"

Professor Brewster pressed something on his tablet.

"This is a feed from it."

He thrust the pad at Kevin, holding it out like an accusation. A buzzing, clicking signal came from it, which sounded as though it might just be static, or a mechanical problem, or crickets stuck somewhere in the workings of the machine.

To Kevin, though, the words were clear.

We are coming. Be prepared to accept us.

CHAPTER SEVEN

"*We?*" Dr. Levin asked. She sounded as though she could barely contain her excitement. "Who is we? Are we talking about some kind of alien civilization?"

"Hold on a second," Professor Brewster snapped, sounding skeptical. "Maybe Kevin's is the wrong translation. Maybe there is nothing to even translate—maybe it's just a bunch of noise. Maybe it's just a figment of the boy's imagination."

"Then how did he know the coordinates?" Dr. Levin asked. "We know that someone sent this signal. Just think of the possibilities..."

She trailed off, as if she couldn't quite comprehend all the possibilities.

"Maybe no one sent it," another scientist piped up. "Space is filled with signals that have no sender, or receiver."

"Still," Dr. Levin insisted, "you can't discount the possibility that this truly is a signal sent by another society. And that Kevin did indeed interpret it directly. What if he did? Are you prepared to shut down that possibility? Are you prepared to just walk away from it? To accept the consequences?"

Brewster fell into a grudging silence.

"We need more information," he finally said. "We need to study Kevin further."

"*Study* him further?" his mother said. "This is my *son*."

"True," Dr. Levin countered. "And yet your son may also just be our planet's sole link to alien life."

*

Kevin sat in the room they had given him and looked around, wondering what it was for. It looked as though it might have been designed for the observation of people over long periods. Either that, or giant goldfish.

It was comfortable, but it was impossible to forget that it was in the middle of the laboratory. The bed was in the middle of the room, and everything seemed to be a pristine, clinical white. Kevin suspected there might be cameras looking down. There was certainly a length of glass along one wall that was obviously one way. It made him feel a little like a frog waiting to be dissected in someone's biology class.

"Do you have everything you need?" his mother asked. "Have they even fed you yet?"

Trust his mother to find a way to be embarrassing even in a situation like this.

"Yes, Mom, they're feeding me," Kevin said.

"I just worry about you," she said.

"You have to work," Kevin said. He understood. His mother couldn't afford to take more time off. Not even for this. There were too many bills to pay, and Kevin being sick had only added medical bills to the list. He didn't like hearing the guilt in his mother's voice, as if she was doing something wrong by taking him to the place where they hunted for aliens.

"This is the best place for you, though," his mother said. She sounded as though she was trying to convince herself.

"It's a cool place to be," Kevin assured her. "They have so many things going on."

It was amazing being a part of something this important.

"Hi, Kevin," Phil said, poking his head around the door. He seemed to brighten even more at the sight of Kevin's mother. "Hi, Ms. McKenzie."

"Call me Rebecca," his mother said. There was something strange in that, maybe because it wasn't something she said very often.

"I thought I would give Kevin the grand tour," Phil said. "Maybe you'd like to join us?"

"That sounds good," his mother said, and again, Kevin had a sense of a side to it that was... no, he shouldn't think like that. That was just gross. Parents weren't supposed to go around *liking* people. That was practically... well, it made the idea of alien worlds look normal.

"If you'd both like to come with me," Phil said, leading the way down the halls. "I mean, officially, I guess we're not supposed to just wander around, because some of the projects are kind of sensitive, but I sometimes think we kind of overdo that, you know?"

He led the way to a space where scientists appeared to be firing a laser at a blank surface again and again, making minute adjustments between each attempt.

"They're looking into ways lasers might be used in mining asteroids," Phil explained. There was something about the look he gave Kevin's mom that said he was trying to impress her. Kevin found that kind of funny. His mom was his mom. She wasn't going to be impressed by *lasers*. Even if they were kind of cool.

After that, he showed them a space where drones flew around in a large room like insects, moving fast but somehow never colliding with one another.

"We're doing work on using AI to make it so that drones can interact without crashing," Phil said.

Kevin saw his mother smile at that. "So that there's less chance of losing the next package I order?"

Phil nodded. "Well, that or they could be used in building work, or for work in extreme environments."

Kevin wasn't sure how he felt about his mom and Phil getting along so well. He was probably supposed to feel happy for her or something, but this was his *mom*. He was sure there were supposed to be rules about that kind of thing. He set off toward another door, hoping to hurry the tour along before the two looked meaningfully into one another's eyes or something.

He opened it, and found himself staring at a thing out of his nightmares.

Kevin staggered back as he found himself face to face with a robot almost as large as he was, covered in spikes and blades, two great pincers sticking out from the front like a hungry ant. It took him a moment to realize that it wasn't moving, wasn't any kind of threat to him in spite of how fierce it looked.

"Is this some kind of weapons project?" Kevin asked. "Something for the military?"

It looked like the kind of thing that would be terrifying coming toward someone on a battlefield. It managed to look pretty terrifying even standing still.

"It's for the local robot fighting league," Phil said. "Some of the grad students from Berkeley come up with vicious stuff."

He looked over at Kevin's mom as if hoping she would declare herself to be a huge fan of robot fighting. When she didn't look particularly impressed, Kevin dared to breathe a sigh of relief. It seemed that the world had returned to normal, kind of.

His mother hugged him. "I have to go, Kevin. I wish I didn't, but…"

Kevin hugged her back. "I know."

Even though he knew she would come back soon, it was hard to let her go.

When she was gone, Kevin turned to Phil. "So," he said. "What now?"

"Now, we have a bunch more tests to get through," Phil said.

A bunch didn't cover it. Even though Phil had tried whole batteries of tests on Kevin before, both Professor Brewster and Dr. Levin seemed determined that they should keep going. Dr. Levin seemed to hope that by understanding what Kevin could do better, they might be able to make more contact with alien civilizations. Professor Brewster... well, Kevin suspected that he hoped it would all prove to be nothing, a mistake.

Either way, it meant test after test with different sets of scientists, question after question, most of which Kevin didn't have the answers to.

"I don't have any control over what I translate," Kevin insisted, when one of the scientists wanted to know if he could look around the alien world he saw to give them more data on it. "I don't even know how I'm doing it. When you play the signals, it's just... obvious."

He suspected the scientists weren't very satisfied with that, but Kevin didn't know what else to say. He got what he got, and for the moment, that seemed to be mostly the countdown in his head, pulsing away ever faster, along with the memory of a world eclipsed by a bright, all-consuming light. So far, it had been the only image he'd gotten. The signal seemed to be just words.

Kevin, needing a break, found a quiet corner in one of the research center's recreation rooms and pulled out his phone and Skyped with Luna.

He smiled when he saw her; he hadn't realized how much he missed seeing her face.

She smiled back.

"Hey, stranger," she said. "They putting you through the mill?"

"Every test you can imagine."

"Being poked and prodded must get pretty bad," Luna said. "But it probably means you're getting looked at by more doctors than you would otherwise. That has to be good, right?"

"I don't think it means that they can do anything for me," Kevin said. He'd thought about this, briefly, but decided he couldn't afford that kind of hope when it came to his illness. He knew what was going to happen. "Most of them aren't even that kind of doctor."

"But some of them must be, and I bet that if there *is* any research into..." Luna looked down, and Kevin guessed that she'd written it down so she wouldn't forget it, "... leukodystrophies, it's going to be somewhere near you."

"If there is, I haven't heard about it," Kevin said. No one had exactly come up to him and told him that there was suddenly a cure for what he had.

"And have you been looking?" Luna asked. She had her determined expression on, the one that meant she wasn't going to take no for an answer.

"I've been too busy trying to translate messages from an alien species," Kevin pointed out.

"Okay," Luna said, "as excuses go, I'll admit that's pretty good. Just think, when they come here and say 'Take me to your leader,' you'll be the only one who can translate, so you'll be there. Your name will be in the history books."

"And when did you last pay attention in history class?" Kevin countered. "I remember trying to help you study for tests, remember?"

"Well, maybe I'd pay more attention if there were more aliens in them."

"Kevin?" Professor Brewster was standing there, looking impatient. "When you're ready, the signal is waiting."

"Looks like I have to go," Kevin said to Luna.

"I miss you," she said, and there was a kind of wistful note to it that wasn't normally there in Luna's voice.

"Well, maybe you could visit," Kevin said, but then he caught sight of Professor Brewster's expression. "I have to go."

"You should be careful about what you say," Professor Brewster said when Kevin hung up. "Our work here is supposed to be confidential."

"I trust Luna," Kevin said.

"And if all of this turns out to be nonsense, then it damages the reputation that we have worked so hard to build up, which in turn will affect our funding."

"It's not nonsense," Kevin insisted. Why couldn't Professor Brewster understand that? "I *see* this."

"Apparently," Professor Brewster said. "Although given your condition…"

Kevin stood up. Right then, he felt tired, and not just because of the illness that was slowly eating away at his brain. He felt tired of all this, of not being taken seriously.

"You're just determined to dismiss this whatever I do," he said. "I managed to translate the message."

"Apparently." That word again. "That reminds me, though. There's no reason to believe that you started listening at the start of these signals, so we want to have you listen to our archive of signals from other sectors, and see if any more trigger sudden translations."

He said that as if he hadn't just barged in, and they weren't having an argument about it. He said it as if it were already decided that Kevin would do it. Kevin stood there, ready to tell him no. Ready to just walk away.

He couldn't, though, and not just because he was thirteen, while this was some eminent scientist who probably knew what he was talking about. He couldn't risk not hearing what the aliens had to say.

"All right," Kevin said.

Professor Brewster took him, not to the supercomputer pit this time, but to a small lab space where there was nothing but a plain white table, a pair of equally plain headphones, and a pane of two-way glass that suggested dozens of scientists might be waiting just beyond.

"Go inside, put the headphones on, and we'll see if any of the signals spark translations," Professor Brewster said in a voice that suggested he knew what the likely outcome would be.

*

The next few hours were among the most boring of Kevin's life, and that included the time he'd spent in math class. Whoever was in the other room played him noise after noise, signal after signal, all presumably interpreted from light patterns or electromagnetic discharges. Kevin expected one of them to spark something at any moment, but there was nothing, and nothing again, and…

"If anyone receives this, more communications will follow," he said as he heard one. It hardly sounded like his voice anymore, as though something were speaking through him. It just seemed natural to say it as the sounds hit his ears.

There seemed to be instant activity behind the glass, and Phil's voice came in on his headphones.

"What was that, Kevin?"

"That last signal, I think it means to wait for more," Kevin said.

"You're sure?"

Kevin didn't know how to answer that. It wasn't as though he was any kind of expert on what was happening. He probably knew less than the scientists trying to make sense of it all. He just translated what he heard, relying on his altered brain to understand.

45

"Maybe if we try for more signals taken from that area," Phil's voice said over the headphones, and Kevin couldn't tell if he was talking to him, or himself, or to other scientists.

Either way, more signals followed. Some were just noise. Others, though…

"We are coming, prepare to receive us."

They were all variations on the same theme, the same message, although none of them seemed to say anything useful. Kevin found himself wondering how long these messages had been pumping out into space, waiting for someone to listen to them. Maybe they'd been striking the Earth for months, even years, and it was only now that someone was able to understand.

Phil seemed to have the same idea. He came in, wearing what looked very much like the same Hawaiian shirt as the day before, looking excited.

"These signals… some of them go back months, maybe longer, all from the region of space we associate with the Trappist 1 system. That means that, if they were sent using light, they've taken almost forty years to arrive. And you're the first person to be able to understand them." Unlike Dr. Brewster, Phil seemed more than happy about the prospect. He sounded truly excited.

"I think your illness must have changed your brain in ways we don't understand," he said. "I think it must have given you the capacity to tune into this in ways we can't. It would explain why we can't see anything beyond the progress of your illness. Your illness is doing this."

Kevin smiled tightly. "So I'm basically a freak."

"But a very important one," Phil said with a smile of his own. "We might have missed understanding this completely. More than that, it sounds as though there's a bigger message coming, something so important that they wanted to be sure no one would miss it."

Kevin thought about the countdown. It was getting faster.

Now, he suspected, he knew what it was counting down to.

The only way to test that was to keep going, working in the institute's testing lab with his headphones on, listening as they pumped in the feed of signals from their listening equipment. He sat there and did his best to translate the signals as Phil sent them through, one by one.

"Nothing with that one," Kevin said, shaking his head.

"I'd have thought there would be *something*," Phil replied, his voice sounding in Kevin's ears as he worked on the other side of a pane of clear glass.

Kevin had thought so too, with the countdown pulsing so fast inside him. Kevin could feel the pulsing, hummingbird fast within him now, impossible to ignore and suggesting that whatever was coming would be here soon. He was tired of waiting, and tired of people staring at him, and sometimes just tired.

"Kevin should take a break." His mother's voice, from outside the room. Kevin was glad she was there. He wasn't sure what that meant for her work, but he was glad she was there.

"I'm sorry, Rebecca, Dr. Brewster was pretty clear that we need to keep feeding Kevin the signal this close to the end of his countdown."

"And are you going to listen to him, or to me?"

Kevin suspected he might be about to get a break. He smiled at that thought. A more worrying one replaced it. What if nothing happened? What if he sat here day after day, and the countdown reached zero without anything happening? What if they'd put this effort in and it was all in vain? How would they all react to that?

A worse thought occurred to him, a thought that made Kevin screw his eyes shut in an attempt to push it away. It didn't work. What if this *was* all his illness? What if the countdown wasn't to a message but to some kind of seizure? What if that too rapid beat was his own heart, or the blood vessels around his brain getting ready to burst? The people of the institute had gathered around Kevin like a prophet about to speak, but what if he really was just dying?

Then the signal came, rushing through him. And he knew the time had come.

***

Kevin could see people rushing to get into the room on the other side, obviously wanting to be there as the message came in. He barely paid any attention to them. The message was too important for that.

"If you are hearing this," Kevin said, translating automatically even though he didn't know how he was doing this, "our world is gone."

He heard the gasps outside as people listened in and realized some of what it must mean. A few of the scientists there started jotting down notes, and Kevin heard them talking in the background.

"That would mean that there haven't been any aliens for at least forty years now," one said.

"*If* there are," another put in. "We only have the kid's word for the translation."

The others ignored him. They seemed as caught up in the moment as Kevin was.

The message kept going, and Kevin kept translating. "We are sending out these messages to preserve what we can of our people, and to ensure that our knowledge does not die."

The signal seemed to intensify, and now it was like a stream that Kevin couldn't have begun to hold back. There were only the strange sounds of the alien language, and the words that came as he translated them almost automatically.

"Our planet was one of seven, with three inhabited. The colonies collapsed first. Home was destroyed in the fires that cleansed it. This is our story, our record. Perhaps hearing it will help others to avoid the same fate as us."

Kevin spoke the words almost without registering the signal that triggered them. The signal was a complex, chattering thing, and if he concentrated, he could just about make out the clicks and buzzes that made it up. Mostly, though, he just got the meaning, pouring straight into his mind as he listened.

It felt as though just keeping his brain locked in with the signal was an effort, and Kevin could feel a bead of sweat forming above his eyes as he worked to keep a grip on it.

"We must send these messages carefully, only a piece at a time, but if you listen, you will learn."

The signal cut out. Kevin waited and kept waiting, listening for more, but there didn't seem to be anything else.

Finally, Kevin looked up. He could see Phil and his mother staring back at him from beyond the glass, but there were others there, plenty of others. Professor Brewster and Dr. Levin were both there, along with as many staff as could fit into the room beyond. He could see the shock on so many of their faces, and he could guess why: they hadn't dared to believe this was real. They'd thought that it would turn into nothing.

This, though, was a long way from nothing.

He could also see their other reason for the shock: they clearly expected the message to continue.

No one had expected it to fall into silence.

CHAPTER EIGHT

Kevin sat very still in Professor Brewster's office while around him, adults tried to work out what all this meant, and what they should do next. Mostly, they did it by talking too much.

Professor Brewster looked surprisingly pleased for once. "That was very impressive, Kevin. I never thought I would see the day. Actual contact with another world! Although we need to be careful, of course. Consider the alternate possibilities."

How did Professor Brewster manage to sound both excited and skeptical at the same time?

"You don't believe it?" Dr. Levin asked.

"We have to consider things carefully," Professor Brewster said. "After all, we don't hear the messages directly, only get translations through a boy who is suffering from a degenerative illness."

"You still think I'm making things up," Kevin said.

"I'm not saying that," Professor Brewster said. "Still... direct contact..."

"I don't think it was direct contact," Kevin said. "It felt... almost like a recorded message."

"If anything, that makes it more plausible," Professor Brewster said. "Because a signal like that would have to travel for years, even moving at the highest speeds. The Trappist 1 system is almost forty light years away, after all."

Kevin knew that. They'd told him before the message had come. He and Phil had discussed it, and he wasn't sure he liked it that Professor Brewster was saying it like it was something he'd just worked out.

Besides, in spite of all that, a part of Kevin had been expecting something else, something live.

"I don't think I got all of it," he said. "I think there's more."

"That doesn't matter, Kevin," his mother said. "The important thing is that you are safe."

"And because you're safe," Professor Brewster added, "you'll be able to pick up more."

The vision had promised that there was more to come. A whole series of messages. A chance to learn everything there was to learn about another world, and Kevin was the key to it.

Some of the others seemed just as excited as he felt.

"We have to publish this," Dr. Levin said.

Professor Brewster held up a hand. "Elise, it's important that we aren't too hasty about that. We have the initial messages, certainly, but we need more before we involve anyone else."

"How much more?" Dr. Levin asked. Kevin could guess why she sounded so frustrated. She'd put her whole life into looking for aliens. Now she had the proof, and of course she would want to shout about it. She wanted people to know, and Kevin... well, he kind of agreed with her.

"Why *can't* we tell people?" Kevin asked. "Why can't we let them know what we found? If I were out there, I'd want to know if people had found aliens."

"It's too early," Professor Brewster insisted. "We should have a full set of data before we announce anything. That way—"

"That way no one can say you're making it up?" Kevin guessed.

To his surprise, his mother spoke up on Professor Brewster's side. "Maybe it's not such a good idea to say anything now, Kevin. We've all seen what you can do, but other people..."

"You think they wouldn't believe me?" Kevin asked.

Professor Brewster nodded. "I think people will need a lot of proof before they believe something like this," he said. "We must be careful to demonstrate to them that this is more than just your imagination, and actually represents an alien communication."

"But I'm translating it," Kevin insisted.

"You appear to be," Professor Brewster said. "We need to establish the patterns between what you're saying and the signals we receive. In the meantime, if we keep it to ourselves, it will prevent a lot of problems."

"What *kind* of problems?" Kevin asked. He couldn't see how something this amazing could be a problem. The news that people weren't alone in the universe sounded incredible to him.

"We do a lot of research here that is considered secret for reasons of national security," Professor Brewster said. "I imagine that my superiors would consider this one of those secrets."

"So you're worried about your *bosses*?" Kevin asked. It didn't seem like a good enough reason to keep from telling people.

"There's also the question of how people might react," Professor Brewster said. "People might panic."

"We understand," Kevin's mother said, putting a hand on Kevin's shoulder.

Kevin didn't understand, though. He didn't see how people would panic at the news that they weren't alone in the universe. To

50

him, it seemed like just about the coolest thing it was possible to learn. He looked over to Dr. Levin, at least expecting support from her. But it seemed that even she was convinced for now.

"I suppose if we wait a while," she said, "that would let us receive more messages."

"They said I could only get a part of the information at once," Kevin said. "Why would they do that? Why not just give it all at once?"

"Maybe they had to do it that way," Dr. Levin said. "Perhaps they had power restrictions, or maybe they wanted to maximize the odds of someone hearing some of it."

"Or maybe they just have that much to send," Professor Brewster suggested. "Like splitting up files when sending email so that the receiver doesn't have to download them in one huge attempt."

That made a kind of sense, although Kevin wasn't sure he liked being referred to as just the receiver. It made him sound as though he was a machine rather than a human being, useful only for what he could do. His mother, or Luna, would never see him like that. If Luna were here, she would see how much it hurt him.

"Either way," Dr. Levin went on hurriedly, "I don't think this is the end of it. What do you think, Kevin? When do you think there might be more?"

Kevin could hear the hope in her voice. This was the kind of moment that her whole career had been working toward, after all. After so long wondering, and maybe hoping, who would be satisfied with just one communication? He would want more, if he were her. He *did* want more. He wanted to hear everything the aliens had to say.

Kevin tried to feel for any sense of the message in its aftermath. The constant pulse of the countdown to the messages wasn't there anymore, but he still had a sense of expectation somewhere deep inside of him that there would be more. The aliens had *said* that, hadn't they?

"I think there will be," he said. It was strange, having so many adults hanging on his words, actually listening to him. He suspected not many thirteen-year-olds got that.

"Then we need to get Kevin back listening to signals," Professor Brewster said.

"David," Dr. Levin said, "Kevin has only just finished translating the first signal. He's also very ill. It isn't right to ask him to plunge back into that without giving him some time to recover."

"But the information—" Professor Brewster began.

"*No one* cares about that more than I do," Dr. Levin said. "I'm not the director over at SETI for nothing. But I also know that you don't learn things by pushing thirteen-year-old boys too hard. Give him time, David. We can record any signals that come from that area of space in the meantime. That will give us a record of them, too."

To Kevin's surprise, Professor Brewster seemed to back down. He hadn't been sure the tall scientist would listen to Dr. Levin on this.

"All right," Professor Brewster said. "We'll give Kevin time to recover. It will allow us to work out the best way to work with this information. But I expect results."

***

Kevin sat listening, trying to pick through the silence for something more. Around him, he could see scientists waiting, some with tablets poised, others with cameras. He could feel the pressure there to perform for them, to do this on command, when the truth was that he could only wait.

There was a kind of rhythm to the waiting, sitting with a set of portable headphones plugged into the stream from the radio telescope. He could feel himself filling with anticipation before the bursts of transmission coming, the feeling like a pulsing in his brain that built in an early warning signal that sent scientists scrambling to record it.

It came now, and Kevin looked up.

"I think there's a message on the way," he said.

It was all that was needed to send scientists hurrying to prepare, most of them moving faster than they moved at any other time. Even so, they were barely in place before the words came through.

"Our civilization started simply, on the fringes of our planet's oceans," Kevin translated. "We spread, and we learned, over many centuries. We built homes. We built cities. We built—"

The transmission cut off, as suddenly as it had started. Kevin waited a moment or two more, in case it would begin again, but it didn't. That seemed to be what it was now: brief bursts and long pauses, with no sign of when it would start again.

Scientists stood around to record everything he was able to give to them, while they made Kevin write down what he could just in case the impressions there were different. Trust scientists to find a way to make something like this feel like *homework*.

It wasn't easy, and not just because some of the researchers seemed to be determined to suck all the fun out of it. Translating took a mental effort, so that Kevin's brain buzzed with it, and he could only stand unsteadily afterward. He hadn't expected this to be physically this hard. Then again, he hadn't expected any of this at all.

"This isn't good for you," Phil said when he saw how shaky Kevin was. "Take your time. Don't push harder than you can push. Not in your condition."

His condition was what made Kevin want to get all he could. It was hard to think about, but how much time did he have now? How many messages would he receive before his brain changed to the point where he couldn't understand them anymore? What if... what if he died before he was done? What if he couldn't get to the end before his body and brain gave way?

It was more than that, though. Every time he sat there translating, listening through his headphones to the latest burst of information, Kevin felt as though all of this might mean something. It was a reminder that he wasn't just a thirteen-year-old boy dying of a disease practically no one had heard of. He was doing something no one else in the history of the world had done. If all of this was *for* something, then that was a good thing.

"I have to keep going," Kevin said. "We need to get all of it."

For the most part, what Kevin managed to pull out were facts, and each one seemed to excite the scientists around him more. Some of it, like the presence of seven planets around the star, or the interlocking gravitational orbits of their moons, were things that they'd been able to work out from their observations using the telescopes available on Earth. Other parts, such as the presence of so much life, had them scratching their heads.

"We think the planets are all tidally locked," one said. "Is there evidence of day shifting into night? If not, one side of the planets should be burning, while the other freezes."

Kevin couldn't tell him at first, until another message explained that yes, the planets spun, in ways that seemed to excite the scientists even more.

"We'll have to rewrite what we know about all of this. What about the radiation exposure from being so close to the star?"

Again and again, they asked questions Kevin didn't know the answers to. They didn't seem to get that he didn't have any control over what the aliens had sent in their bursts of messages. They sent what they sent, Kevin translated it, and the scientists had to scramble to try to make some kind of sense of it.

Strangely, Dr. Levin was the one person who didn't seem to mind that.

"It's just astonishing that they've chosen to communicate in this way," she said. "They're sending so much information about themselves, trying to preserve some understanding of who they are."

"Who they *were*," Kevin corrected her. That was one thing that the messages had been clear about. The people sending them were long gone. That was both incredibly sad and also kind of cool, knowing that he was pretty much the last link to a dead civilization.

One strange thing was how simple and factual it all was. Kevin had been kind of expecting to learn more about the culture or the languages of the beings that inhabited the planet, yet he still hadn't seen enough of them to understand what they really were. Which of the creatures on the planet's surface were they? Were they the chitin-shelled creatures that crawled there, or the long-necked things like scaled giraffes? Kevin's imagination kept him expecting something humanlike and familiar, but so far he hadn't heard any reference to it.

Kevin just wished that he could share more of those words with the world. When he couldn't stand it any longer, he sought out Dr. Levin, because he suspected she would be his biggest ally. He found her in the canteen with Phil.

"I'm worried that I'm saying all of this, and it's just going to be locked away in secret somewhere," he said.

"Professor Brewster is just being careful," Dr. Levin said. To Kevin, she sounded as though she was trying to convince herself.

"What if he's so careful no one ever learns about the aliens?" Kevin asked. It was a real worry. He could imagine the tall scientist doing it all too easily. "What if my mother only agrees because she doesn't want people laughing at me?"

"I'm sure that won't happen," Dr. Levin said. Again, she didn't sound sure.

"What aren't you telling me?" Kevin asked. He wasn't sure if Dr. Levin would answer that or not.

"David… Professor Brewster… has to answer to people inside the government," Dr. Levin said. "Some of his funding is from the military. Something like this… they might want to keep it secret."

Kevin could tell she wasn't happy about that. "So he might *never* tell people?"

"They'd probably be worried about people panicking," Dr. Levin said. Again, Kevin got the feeling that she didn't agree.

54

"*You* must want to tell people," Kevin said. "Your whole organization wants to find aliens."

Dr. Levin smiled tightly. "I can't," she said. "If I do, it will make things harder for SETI. Professor Brewster wouldn't let it go, and some of his bosses… well, they'd see it as a betrayal."

"Even though people have a right to know?" Kevin said.

"They'd say that people only have a right to know what they're told," Dr. Levin said.

Kevin shook his head. "This isn't right. Professor Brewster shouldn't do this."

"I'll try talking to him. In the meantime, Phil, why don't you take Kevin for a walk around the facility? I'm sure it must be pretty boring spending all your time either here or in your room."

It was, in ways that made even school seem interesting by comparison. Kevin might never have been one of those kids who went to a different activity every night, and camp in the summer, but he'd never spent his time in one room either, doing nothing but acting as a kind of human satellite dish for alien messages.

He'd been around the facility before, but it was good to spend some time being something other than the kid who heard the messages. Phil led the way, using his security access. Despite effectively living there now, Kevin didn't have any. Apparently, they could trust him enough to receive alien signals, but not to be able to come and go as he wanted.

"We're working on producing plants that can survive in extreme environments," Phil said, pointing to a room full of what appeared to be tomato plants. "Maybe if all of this leads to humanity *meeting* aliens, we'll be able to offer them a nice plant to take home."

Kevin smiled at that thought. "The aliens are dead, remember? They said that their planet was destroyed."

"But *someone* must have sent that signal," Phil said. "So they must have survived to do it."

"I guess," Kevin said, but even so, he wasn't hopeful. What if they'd just survived long enough to send out their messages? What if they'd lived out lives of a few more years, only to die on some far-off world? The contact with the aliens felt almost as doomed in the long run as everything else about his life.

"And this elevator leads down to the bunker," Phil said, gesturing to a set of doors.

"A bunker?" Kevin said. "Like, a nuclear bunker?"

"Nuclear, chemical, biological," Phil said. "The idea is to have one close by in the event that there ever is some kind of war, or attack, or something. There are bunkers all over the place, and they give some senior people keys to save the 'best and the brightest' if it looks as though the world will end."

He didn't sound particularly happy about the idea. Maybe he suspected that he wouldn't be on the list.

"So these bunkers are everywhere?" Kevin said.

Phil nodded, then took out his phone. "There's a whole map of them," he said. "Although Professor Brewster doesn't know I have this."

He showed Kevin the map, covered in small red dots. There was one right under them, and another tucked away to the east in the state park under Mount Diablo.

"That seems like a strange place for a bunker," Kevin said.

"It's because it's away from the city," Phil replied. "It means it's more likely to survive an attack. Besides, no one talks about it, but they used to do military testing up there."

It sounded like the kind of secret Kevin wasn't supposed to know, but then, he suspected that *aliens* were the kind of secret he wasn't supposed to know right then.

"I guess I wouldn't make it into one of the bunkers anyway," Kevin said. He couldn't help a note of resentment there.

"Still angry that the professor decided to keep you a secret here?" Phil asked.

Kevin was about to say no, say the thing he was supposed to say, but the truth was that he *was* angry.

"He can't just do that," Kevin said. "The aliens are sending a message to the whole world. Shouldn't everyone get to hear it?"

Phil shrugged. "The trouble is, he can. Especially if his bosses want to keep anything you do for military applications. This is a facility that engages in confidential research, and it has plenty of security. Keeping people out is easy. Keeping secrets in, though…"

"What do you mean?" Kevin asked.

The researcher gestured for him to follow, and he led the way to a broad window near the front entrance to the building, looking out over the research facility's front lot. Out beyond the fence, where the public part of the NASA facility stood, Kevin could see a large crowd of people all looking toward the building. Several of them had cameras.

"Who are they?" Kevin asked.

"Someone must have let it slip that we were working on something to do with aliens," Phil said, in a tone that suggested exactly who that someone might be. "Probably a scientist who decided that you shouldn't keep things like this quiet."

"Or you," Kevin suggested, because he'd never really understood it when adults tried to say things without actually saying them, like that.

"It could have been your mother," Phil pointed out, "and Dr. Levin would *love* to be able to tell the public about extraterrestrial life being real. I mean, it's literally her job. Or—"

"But it wasn't them," Kevin said. "It was you, wasn't it?"

"Shh," Phil said. "Do you want to cost me my job? Now, it occurs to me that, if you were to go out there and talk to those people, old Brewster wouldn't be *able* to keep you locked away. I'm just talking hypothetically, you understand."

Kevin looked over at the doors. They were solid things, with a card lock for which he didn't have a card. They seemed like an impossible barrier. Even the glass beside them was toughened.

"I can't get outside," he said.

"Why would you need to get outside?" Phil replied, with an expression of badly feigned shock. "I'm just talking hypothetically. I hope you understand that if I did anything to help you, Kevin, I could get into a lot of trouble."

"I... think I understand," Kevin said, with a slight frown, because he wasn't quite sure that he did. Seriously, why didn't people say what they meant?

"Oh," Phil said, "I just remembered, I was supposed to help fix a security problem with the cameras in front of the doors."

"What security problem?" Kevin asked with a frown.

"The one that's going to happen in about two minutes. *Someone* is going to decide it would be a good idea to let one of the experimental AIs play chess with them. Incidentally, could you do me a favor, Kevin?"

Kevin looked over at him. "What do you need?"

Phil took out what looked very much like a keycard. "Professor Brewster dropped this. Would you mind returning it to him when you see him? I'm sure he'll be along to demand answers from you at some point."

Kevin took it. "I will," he said. "And Phil... thank you."

"For what?" the researcher asked. "I didn't do anything. Actually, it's quite important to remember that part."

"I will," Kevin promised.

As Phil walked away, Kevin forced himself to wait, counting the seconds under his breath. He saw the lights on the cameras by the door go dim, and quickly swiped the card in the door.

He walked out from the building, feeling strange being out in the open air for the first time in days. The air in the facility was so pristine, so carefully filtered, that it felt almost stale next to this. It felt strange to be walking like this too, when he'd spent so much time sitting or lying down, doing nothing but relaying the contents of that golden thread of information. He kept walking, then ran, as he heard a shout behind him. He glanced back to see a security guard there, looking unsure what to do next and speaking into a radio.

Kevin kept going for the fence, not sure how much more time he would have.

Professor Brewster was somewhere behind him now, yelling for him to come back. Kevin smiled at that. It would only make it more likely that people would believe what he was going to do next. It might mean that people *listened*.

He ran up to the fence and stopped, looking at the people there, looking at the cameras. Some were from local news stations. At least a couple seemed to be from national ones. Faced with that, Kevin swallowed nervously. He didn't know what to say.

"Um... hi, I'm Kevin. You've probably heard some of the rumors about what's been going on here? Well, they're true."

CHAPTER NINE

Kevin sat in Professor Brewster's office, getting the feeling that the scientist would love to shout at him, if only he had enough time. He certainly looked angry enough to do it. Frankly, right then, he looked just about angry enough to explode. He *didn't* have enough time, though, because he was too busy answering phone calls, trying to talk to Kevin and Dr. Levin in between.

"Yes sir. Yes, I'm sure it is. Yes, it's true that the boy seems to be... yes, yes, of course. But sir, it's our project and... yes sir, of course I'm aware of the implications." He put the phone down. "That was the director of NASA. Can you understand how difficult this is, Kevin? How complicated this is about to—"

He picked up the phone again as it rang.

"Hello? Who? No, I'm sorry. No. *No*, I don't accept that the boy should be taken into FBI custody for his own safety."

He put the phone down.

"This is only the start of it," he said. He looked over to Kevin. "Do you understand, Kevin, that part of the reason I wanted to keep this a secret was because I knew how some people would react? News of alien life is a big thing for this country, for the world. I wanted to protect you from all the different people who would want to try to control part of that."

Kevin stared at the older man. He hadn't thought that Professor Brewster was interested in much beyond the success of his institute. It was strange to think that he might have been trying to look out for him. Adults, he decided, were far too complicated.

The phone rang again.

"The CIA? But we're on American... Yes, I accept that space is beyond American borders, but..."

While they were busy arguing about it, Dr. Levin put a hand on his shoulder.

"How about we take you back to your room, Kevin?" she suggested. "I'm sure they'll be arguing for a while yet."

Kevin nodded, and they slipped off. He wasn't sure if Professor Brewster noticed, he was that busy fielding calls. Briefly, he wondered what would happen if he just walked out of the facility again and kept walking, not coming back. Would the scientist do anything to stop him? Would he be able to?

A glance out the window suggested that wouldn't be easy. Already, the crowd of reporters had swollen until it seemed like a horde of them wanting to get in, the security on site barely enough to keep them back. That security looked as though it was about to be reinforced, though, because military vehicles were rolling up, spreading out around the perimeter of the facility, with armed men jumping out.

"All this because I talked about aliens on TV?" Kevin said. It seemed like a lot, given the number of people who did that.

"All this because we *proved* aliens to them," Dr. Levin corrected him, and Kevin guessed that far fewer people had done that. "There will be a lot more."

"How many more?" Kevin asked. He wasn't sure he was comfortable with the idea of being surrounded just because he'd said something.

"Follow me." She led the way over to one of the recreation rooms. The TV there was on, scientists staring at one of the news channels.

"The boy, identified as Kevin McKenzie of Walnut Creek, California, claimed to be in contact with an extraterrestrial source of information, and gave extensive details about the Trappist 1 planetary system, believed by many experts to be—"

Dr. Levin flipped the channel, and now there was an interview there with a wild-eyed man in a grubby T-shirt for a band Kevin didn't know.

"It's all a lie," he said. *"It's a distraction. The government wants us looking at this, so that we're not looking at the truth! It's an excuse, so that when they start drugging the drinking water, it will all seem normal!"*

Dr. Levin flipped the channel again. Now, there was a pastor on the screen talking in front of a large congregation.

"It's clear that what the boy is actually hearing is the voice of God, preparing us for the Rapture! We must be—"

She turned the TV off, ignoring the protests of the scientists as she did so.

"That's enough," she said. "You all have work to do, and it will be complicated enough now without listening to all that trash. You know the truth. You've seen it. Get back to work."

To Kevin's surprise, they did, even though Dr. Levin wasn't their boss. Maybe they were just looking for someone to tell them what to do. He knew he was, right then. He might understand the aliens' messages, but he wasn't sure that he really got what half of this might mean.

"Things are going to get tricky," Dr. Levin said to him. "There will be people now trying to twist what you say, and use it for their own ends."

"So what do *I* do?" Kevin asked.

She shrugged. "Just keep saying things exactly as you see them. You're at the heart of something big, but you need tell the truth, do your best with it. It's all any of us can hope to do right now."

Kevin nodded, but he doubted that it would be that easy. At least one reason it wouldn't be easy was his mom, and she was standing across the recreation room from him now. He found that he was afraid. What would she say? He knew she'd been almost as eager to keep the secret of all of this as Professor Brewster, and yet he'd told people everything.

She rushed forward to hug him. "Kevin, are you all right? I thought they'd bring you back to your room, and then I went to Professor Brewster's office and he was on the phone to the Pope, and…"

"I'm fine, Mom," Kevin assured her. Right then, he would have said it even if he weren't, just to take away some of the look of worry on her face.

"There are so many people out there now," she said. "Kevin, we were just trying to keep you safe."

Kevin shook his head. It was important that people knew about what was happening. It didn't matter if he was safe. "I had to tell them."

"And now I think they're going to go crazy out there if somebody doesn't tell them more," his mother said.

Dr. Levin cocked her head to one side, then looked out at the crowds beyond the building. "Your mother has a point, Kevin. Someone needs to explain all this to people."

"What did you have in mind?" Kevin asked.

"I think we need to organize a press conference."

***

"We need to be very careful about this," Professor Brewster said, as he, Kevin, and Dr. Levin stepped into one of the institute's conference rooms together. "I'm only agreeing to this because the alternative is letting people make up what they want in place of the truth."

Kevin guessed that he didn't like the idea of people trying to force their way into his research center to learn the truth, either.

"So we tell them the truth," Kevin said.

To his surprise, he saw Professor Brewster shake his head. "Ideally, Kevin, I think it's best if you say as little as possible. We need to manage people's expectations of all this and what it might mean for them."

"But there are *aliens*," Kevin said.

"And that will scare a lot of people," Professor Brewster explained. "We need to be careful. Trust me, I've been involved in announcing a lot of scientific discoveries. It's important to get the message right with these things so that people can understand the potential implications of it all."

He led the way out to a small platform, where some of the researchers had set up a small table. Kevin sat in the middle, with the two adults flanking him. Out in front of him was what seemed to be a sea of people, many of them with cameras. They started to shout questions almost as soon as Kevin and the others sat down.

"Professor Brewster, have you really found evidence of alien life?"

"Can we expect to be visited by aliens in the near future?"

"Is this all some kind of joke?"

"Who is the boy?"

Kevin did his best to just sit there, while Professor Brewster leaned forward and started to answer, looking officious.

"Well, those are all very complex questions," the institute's director began, and Kevin could see how this was going to go.

Apparently, so could Dr. Levin. "Yes," she said. "There are aliens. No, this is not a joke, and most of you have already met Kevin. From what I've seen of the news, half of you have already started to trawl through his life. There's really no point. We're not trying to hide anything. To prove that, we're going to hold regular press conferences here, explaining what we find out."

Professor Brewster looked as though he'd swallowed something unpleasant, but the questions were already coming in again.

"But does the boy, does *Kevin*, really have communications with an alien civilization?" a reporter called out. "He's talking to them?"

When Dr. Levin looked over to him, Kevin stood up, trying not to look as nervous as he felt right then.

"I'm not talking to aliens," he said. "I've had… some visions, I guess… and I can translate their signal when I hear it. That's all."

"That's all?" a reporter said, with a laugh "It sounds like plenty. Will *we* get to hear these signals?"

"I'm not sure anyone would understand them," Kevin said. Although what if someone did? What if there was someone else out there like him? Would that be a good thing or a bad thing? Kevin didn't know right then.

"But we have you to translate, don't we?" another reporter called out. "Doesn't the public have a right to hear these messages?"

"They do," Dr. Levin said, and again, Kevin had the impression of her speaking up before Professor Brewster could say anything. "Which is why we'll be holding regular press conferences from now on, where Kevin will try to decipher the signals we've recorded from that region."

Professor Brewster stood up. He had a smile fixed in place that looked as though it might crack at any moment. "Okay, folks. I think we shouldn't tire out Kevin too much. That's enough for one day."

***

This time, Professor Brewster had more than enough time to shout.

"You ambushed me, Elise!" Professor Brewster said. "Regular press conferences?"

"Come on, David," Dr. Levin said. "You know it's the right thing to do, and this way you get to keep everything orderly, rather than having people trying to break in to get information. You're a scientist. You don't believe in hiding things away."

"I also don't believe in getting our funding cut because someone in Congress thinks I'm giving away something we should hold onto," Professor Brewster said, and Kevin could hear some of the worry under the anger.

Kevin wondered what it must be like to have Professor Brewster's job. Presumably, he'd wanted to be a scientist when he was Kevin's age, had wanted to discover things. Now, it seemed as though he mostly spent his time organizing things and worrying about money. It sounded like the kind of thing someone had to do if they were a manager or something, not a scientist. It wasn't something Kevin would have wanted to have to do.

"We've announced them now," Dr. Levin said.

"You've announced them," Professor Brewster said. "We can still—"

He found himself interrupted by a call, and something about his expression as he answered said that this was different from the calls he'd received so far about this.

"Hello? Yes, this is he… I'm sorry, did I hear you correctly?… Yes, at once." He looked ashen as he put the phone down. "We need to go to the lobby, now."

"Why?" Kevin asked.

"Because they're saying that the President is here."

Kevin might have asked if he was joking, but one look at Professor Brewster's face made it obvious he wasn't. Kevin's heart tightened in his chest at the thought. The President was coming here, to see him? Somehow, even the presence of the aliens seemed more possible than that. Kevin suddenly found himself wondering if he'd just done the right thing, nerves rising up through him. It didn't seem right somehow that *he* was meeting the *President*.

He followed Professor Brewster and Dr. Levin to the research institute's lobby, having to hurry to keep up. It was obvious that they didn't to keep the President waiting. As they got closer, Kevin glanced out of the building's windows, seeing a long motorcade there, full of vehicles with blacked out windows.

By the time they reached the lobby, the President was already in the building, and he wasn't the only one. Secret Service agents in dark suits spread out as if expecting a threat at any moment. Advisors and assistants trailed him in a huddle, some of them looking a little surprised that they were there. Kevin saw other people too, with badges proclaiming them to be from the military, the NSA, the FBI, and more. It seemed that no one had wanted to miss out on being a part of this.

The President walked over as they arrived, taking Professor Brewster's hand, then turning his attention to Kevin. Kevin swallowed nervously as the older man stared at him.

"So this is the boy?" the President said, looking Kevin up and down as if expecting far more.

"Yes, sir," Professor Brewster said, sounding positively deferential. "This is Kevin."

"Kevin? All right, Kevin, do you know who I am?"

"You're the President," Kevin said. Inside, a small voice was repeating the words *you're talking to the President* over and over. He did his best to ignore it, because if he listened too much, he suspected that he might not be able to say anything.

"Good lad. Now, tell me honestly, can you really talk to aliens?"

"No sir," Kevin said.

"Ha, I knew it!" the President said. "I told them in the emergency contingencies committee that—"

"I can't talk to them, but I do receive messages from them," Kevin went on. "They send information about themselves and their planet, and I can translate it."

The President's expression changed, as if he didn't quite know what to say to that. Kevin was getting used to that expression from people by now.

"Well then," the President said, wagging a finger. "Just you remember that this information was given to us, in America. It was obviously intended for us as the most advanced nation on Earth."

"Sir," Professor Brewster said, "the signal hits the whole world. Kevin is just the one who is able to translate it. You should also be aware that we've agreed to press conferences so that we can't be accused of hiding the information."

Kevin was surprised to find the man sticking up for sharing the information like that. Sticking up for *him* like that. An advisor came up to the President and whispered something in his ear.

"Well," the President said, "maybe that's a good thing. Other countries will see us sharing it and know that they wouldn't have gotten it without us."

"Yes, sir," Professor Brewster said.

"But now, I'd like to see a demonstration. Kevin, can you show me what you can do?"

Kevin looked to the others, who nodded. "We can only do it if there's a signal," he said.

But even as he said it, he could feel the pressure in his skull that preceded one. An alarm sounded and they hurried in the direction of the room where he did the translating, sitting and waiting. Kevin sat there, while outside the President and his advisors stood around, looking as though they didn't know what was happening.

Words filtered into his mind, the translation happening automatically.

Our world was destroyed. The words sounded flat, without emotion. *We had to flee. So few survived.*

Kevin repeated the words, and he could see the President's expression changing, first to surprise, and then to something like wonder.

We hid everything we were, the voice said, and Kevin repeated it, *as much of ourselves as we could before the fire came. Messages were sent out, so that people would know of us. We sent capsules in every direction, toward all of the inhabited worlds.*

65

Kevin tried to imagine it, spaceships sent in every direction, trying to find safety. How much effort would it have taken to organize that? How would they have been able to organize it with a disaster threatening them?

Each vessel holds a record of our history, the voice continued.

Coordinates will be sent along this path, the voice said, *but the vessel's seal will be tight to preserve us. You must find it. You must prepare to receive us…*

Kevin gasped with the effort of translating, the world around him coming into focus again as he stopped. He could see the President staring at him now, then looking over to Professor Brewster.

"What does all this mean?" he asked. "What are you telling me?"

Kevin could answer that one.

"I think…" Kevin said. "I think the aliens are coming here."

The President stared at him. So did the others. Then the chaos started, with a dozen people trying to talk at once. The President spoke over them.

"That's enough," he said, gesturing for them to quiet down. "I know all of your concerns. Professor Brewster, there are those on my team who feel that Kevin here isn't safe in your facility; that he is vulnerable to being snatched or attacked by our enemies. They want to move him to a secure site."

"You mean you want to hide me away in some kind of bunker," Kevin said. He shook his head. "I don't want to do that."

"Sometimes it isn't about what we want, son," the President said. "It's about what's good for the country."

"With respect, Mr. President," Professor Brewster said. "Kevin's wishes on the matter *should* count for something. He has not committed a crime, so it would be wrong, even illegal, to lock him up. This is a secure facility, and if the others here want to contribute to that security, that would be very helpful. But they should do that *here*, where there is the technological knowhow to study what is happening."

Kevin was surprised to find Professor Brewster standing up for him like that, even if he knew that it was partly because he didn't want to risk losing the chance to be a part of all this. It seemed that the President was a little surprised to hear it too.

"That's a very… forceful point, Professor," he said. "Very well, the boy will stay here. We will provide your facility with whatever it needs, but you *will* coordinate with my office. I need you to understand the seriousness of this."

"Yes sir," Professor Brewster said. "Thank you, Mr. President."

Kevin wasn't entirely sure what the professor had just agreed to. It sounded as though he'd just given away a lot of the control of the project.

"I need *you* to understand the seriousness of this too, Kevin," the President said. "I thought before I came here that this was nonsense, and now I'm not so sure."

"It's true," Kevin insisted.

"The truth is that it doesn't matter," the President said. "Not now. We have reports of Russia and China mobilizing their militaries, conducting 'exercises' in case of some kind of attack. There have been riots in the Philippines, because people think this means the end of the world. We need to be very careful about all this, Kevin. I'm going to allow things to continue for now, but there *will* be people here to watch what's happening."

That didn't matter to Kevin. What mattered was that they kept going. The aliens were sending something to Earth, and whatever it was, Kevin was determined to find it.

CHAPTER TEN

Kevin sat in his room, listening to nothing. There were signals, recorded by the scientists through their long-range equipment, but none of those signals turned into words within his mind. None of them seemed to have meaning.

Kevin was starting to get worried about that, and it seemed that he wasn't the only one.

"Why aren't you hearing anything, Kevin?" Professor Brewster asked. He and Dr. Levin stood there watching, waiting for whatever would come next.

Kevin didn't have an answer. "I don't know. Maybe there's nothing to listen to."

"You must *try,* Kevin," Professor Brewster said, with a disapproving look, as if the solution to it lay in simply doing more, or pushing past the difficulty of contact.

"David," Dr. Levin said. "Don't pressure Kevin. Can't you see that he's getting sicker?"

Kevin knew that part was true. He'd started to notice a small tremor now in his left hand that would stop if he concentrated, but quickly started again whenever he was stressed. That meant most of the time now in the research institute.

"Then we need to get him more medical attention," Professor Brewster declared. "Kevin, you have to understand, I have government departments I've barely even heard of calling me up to know what's happening. I had a four-star general call me earlier, wanting to know if there were any potential military applications for this information. With the President wanting to know what's happening, this isn't a good time for us not to be able to say anything."

"I can't translate things if they aren't there," Kevin said. What did they want him to do? Make things up? Maybe they still thought he was doing that, despite everything. Kevin hated that thought.

"Maybe you just need a break," Dr. Levin said. "Go for a walk around the institute, try to relax a little, and we can get back to listening for signals later, when you've rested a little."

Kevin nodded, and went out into the institute, deciding to go search out his mother. When she wasn't in his room now, she was usually somewhere near where Phil was working, or in the small space the research center had given her so that she could stay near

Kevin. Kevin decided to check there first, and set off along the halls.

There seemed to be more people in the research institute now than there had been before. Kevin could see people in military uniforms and others in suits wearing earpieces. A trio wearing NSA badges stopped as Kevin went past, looking at him as if wondering how he was allowed to just wander the halls like that.

One of the stranger people there was a man who looked to be in his forties, with the short-cropped hair and erect posture of some of the military people, even though he was wearing a leather jacket and jeans instead of a uniform, and clearly hadn't shaved for a week.

"You're wondering who I am," he said, as Kevin stared at him.

Kevin nodded nervously. He suspected some people wouldn't react too well to being stared at like that.

"You have good instincts," he said. "The number of scientists who have walked past me without wondering that... with so many people going in and out, *anyone* could get in here if they aren't careful."

"Anyone?" Kevin asked. "Who are you?"

"I'm Ted," he said, extending a hand. A group of soldiers went past and Ted nodded to them. To Kevin's surprise, one of them gave him a brief salute.

"Are you with the military?" Kevin asked. "The CIA? The police?"

"Something like that," Ted said. He thought for a moment. "Actually, *nothing* like that, these days. And you're Kevin, the kid who can decipher the alien signals."

He was probably the first person who'd gotten that right. Most of them seemed to think that he was getting a live stream from an alien civilization, or could actually talk to them. That part made him want to stop and talk to this man, but even so, there was something about his presence there that made Kevin pause. He didn't fit in.

"I'm sorry," Kevin said. "I need to get going."

"That's fine, Kevin," the man said. "I'm sure we'll see one another again."

Kevin hurried off. He could practically feel Ted watching him as he went. He found his mother in the small bedroom that the institute had provided her with so she could stay close.

"Kevin, are you all right?" she asked. "You look a bit pale."

"I'm okay," Kevin said. "Mom, there's a man out there, and I'm not sure..."

He staggered slightly as the room swam. One moment he was upright; the next, he was on the floor, with people surrounding him. It took Kevin a second or two to realize that he must have had a seizure. There were medical staff there, and researchers, and of course his mother, but no sign of the man who had been there before.

"I'm okay," Kevin said, struggling to sit up. He still felt dizzy, though, and only his mother's arm around him stopped him from falling back again.

"You're not okay," she said. "Come on, we'll get you back to your room, and then I'm going to ask Professor Brewster why he isn't taking care of my baby."

"*Mom*," Kevin managed, because he *wasn't* a baby, he was thirteen. Even so, he let his mother help him back in the direction of his room. Somewhere along the line, Phil joined them, the two more or less propping Kevin up between them until they could get him back to his bed.

"I'm going to go find out why they aren't looking after your health better than this," his mother said, and she set off with the determined look of someone who needed to get angry about something before she started crying.

"I guess we should work out exactly what's happening," Phil said, as she left. "What do you say, Kevin? Are you up for some more tests?"

"*More* tests?" Kevin countered.

There were, because Phil wanted to get an MRI, and then bloodwork. Kevin had only realized in the last couple of weeks just how much he hated having needles poked into him, because it seemed that everyone wanted his blood for something. Researchers and medical staff came and went, all explaining what they were doing as they went about it, almost none of them using words that Kevin could actually understand.

"We've made advances with anti-seizure medication," one of the nurses told Kevin, "but the doctors are currently in discussions with all the people here, asking if it's the best thing."

Meaning that they were worried it might block off his ability to understand the signal, whenever it next showed up. Kevin could imagine them there, trying to balance the possibility of missing the information that might lead to the aliens against the possibility that Kevin might die and never give them anything else. Probably only a few of them would think about what it all meant for him, and so far, none of them had thought to ask what treatment he wanted.

"*Is* it the best thing?" Kevin asked.

70

The nurse shrugged. "Officially, I'm not supposed to have an opinion on that. Unofficially… I hear a couple of the doctors are talking about using variations on gene therapies developed for people with other illnesses, like Alexander's syndrome."

"I didn't think there was anything like that available for me," Kevin said, thinking back to the consultation with Dr. Markham, and all the ones that had followed it.

"There hasn't been, but you currently have most of the biggest brains in the country on your side. If anyone can tailor something to your condition, it's them."

And then Kevin would find himself taking an experimental treatment that might cure him, might do nothing, or might make things worse. Would that be worth the risk of losing the alien signal completely?

"For the moment, though, you have a visitor."

She nodded to the doorway and the short figure coming through it. Kevin's eyes widened at the sight of Luna, looking as casual as if she'd just called around to his house to see if he wanted to ride bikes down to the reservoir.

"Luna? How did you get here?"

"My mom brought me along," Luna said with a smile. "Because *your* mom thought you'd like to see me." She held up an orange, then threw it to him. "I didn't have any grapes."

Kevin caught it clumsily while Luna perched on the edge of his bed. Her expression changed from happy to see him to worried.

"How bad is it?" she asked, most of her usual cheerfulness gone from her voice.

"I don't know," Kevin said. He glanced away for a moment. "Well, I guess we kind of *do* know."

Luna put a hand on his shoulder. "They might have said that you're going to die, but I refuse to let you die *yet*, Kevin. I haven't even fallen madly in love with you yet."

Kevin laughed at that. "If I have to wait for that, I might live forever."

"True," Luna said, but her smile didn't reach her eyes. Kevin could see how much it hurt her having to be strong for him, having to be cheerful.

"It's okay to cry if you want to," Kevin said.

"As if I'm going to cry," Luna said, although she looked like she might for a moment.

She *didn't* cry, but she did hug him, hard enough that Kevin thought his ribs might break. He surprised himself by noticing how good she smelled.

"I've missed you, you know?" she said.

"I've missed you too," Kevin assured her. He'd told her that it was okay to cry, but now he was the one with tears stinging the corners of his eyes.

"Hey, I shouldn't make you upset," Luna said. "One of the military guys in the hall would probably shoot me if I did that."

That was enough to make Kevin laugh. Luna had always had the knack of doing it.

"What's it like out there?" he asked. "Out in the real world? What's it like at school, or on TV? I'm sick of everything just being about the things I can see for people."

"Sorry to disappoint you," Luna said. "But there's plenty about you on TV. There are reporters at your house most days now, and people talking about whether this is real, or a hoax, or an advertising campaign that got out of hand. There's even a weird alien cult that has started up, people wearing antennae as they walk around and claiming that the aliens will save us from everything from environmental breakdown to high grocery prices."

"You're making that up," Kevin guessed.

"Maybe the part about the antennae," Luna said. She looked around. "It must be peaceful being here. It's really quiet."

"It's been a lot busier since people found out what I could do," Kevin said. "And I spend most of my time listening for the signals, so it's not exactly a library."

Luna smiled the smile of someone who usually did all the talking they wanted in libraries anyway.

It didn't stay quite that peaceful, either, because Professor Brewster, Dr. Levin, and Kevin's mother all came in together.

"You're pushing Kevin too hard," his mother was saying.

"We're really not trying to, Rebecca," Dr. Levin assured her. "We don't have any control over the signals we receive, and Kevin is able to stop whenever he needs to."

"And Kevin has barely listened to any today," Professor Brewster said. "Besides, he's receiving better treatment here than he would be able to get anywhere else in the country."

"That's... true," his mother admitted. She sounded pretty reluctant to do it though.

"We *are* looking after your son," the institute's director continued. "And Kevin is doing important work here. Speaking of which, Kevin, do you feel up to facing the cameras?"

"Now?" Kevin asked. He wasn't sure.

"There have been some rumors that you're unwell today, and it seems like a good idea to show people that you're healthy," Professor Brewster said.

"Even though he isn't?" Luna asked, beside Kevin.

"Especially because of that," Professor Brewster said. "And anyway, people are waiting to hear more of what Kevin has to say. Kevin?"

"You don't have to do it," his mother said.

Kevin nodded. "It's okay. I'm feeling a lot better now. If it will help, I'll do it."

***

Kevin felt as though standing up in front of people should get easier. He wasn't doing anything, after all, that he hadn't already done before. He'd shown them what he could do at the gates to the facility, and in a press conference before. Even so, he was nervous with so many people staring back at him.

"It will be fine," Luna said. How did she always seem to guess when he was feeling bad? "And you can't back out now. I want to watch you do your alien stuff."

"Alien stuff," Kevin repeated. "We definitely need a better name for it than that."

Even so, he stepped out to face the crowd. There were more people here today, cramming every corner of the conference room where Kevin was due to perform for them. There were reporters, obviously, scientists, government people...

...and Ted, staring at him intently from the crowd.

"That guy's here," Kevin said.

"What guy?" Luna asked.

"I met him in the halls while I was looking for my mom, and he just seemed... I don't know, out of place. He kind of seemed like he might have been one of the soldiers, but he said he wasn't anymore. I don't even know if he's supposed to be here."

"You think he's some crazy guy?" Luna asked. "You think he's here to kill everyone?"

"I didn't until you said it," Kevin said. Now that she had, Kevin found his eyes locked onto the spot where Ted stood. He wondered if he should tell someone about him.

"Time to do your stuff, Kevin," Professor Brewster said, nudging him toward the center of the platform they'd set up. "Hello, everyone, as you can see, Kevin is fine, and some of the rumors out there are greatly exaggerated."

"What rumors?" Kevin asked him, and then found his eyes pulled back to Ted again. "Professor Brewster, there's this man out there…"

Professor Brewster ignored him. "Kevin is quite tired today, though, so we'll keep this short. Kevin?"

Kevin stepped forward and put his headphones in place, figuring that it was probably best to just get on with this. The trouble was that there was still silence, nothing new to translate, no signal coming in. He stood there in silence for several seconds, feeling increasingly embarrassed. Worse, he couldn't take his eyes off Ted, convinced that the moment he did, the man would do something.

That was when a completely different man, toward the front of the hall, started shouting. "You're evil!" he yelled. "You'll bring the aliens down on all of us!"

He ran forward, and even though he had a press pass, and was dressed smartly in a suit, there was something wild in his eyes. He charged at the stage, and Kevin saw him shove Luna out of the way as he went, sending her sprawling to the ground.

"Luna!" Kevin shouted, but there was no time to help her, because the man was still coming, and now Kevin could see that he had a knife. He grabbed Kevin, and the next moment, the man was behind him, the blade pressed to Kevin's throat.

"You're trying to bring them here. You're trying to let them destroy us all. I have to stop you, whatever it takes."

Kevin had never been so frightened before, but the strangest part was that most of that fear wasn't for himself. Luna was lying still where the man had knocked her down, and now Kevin was wondering if he might have stabbed her, just because she got in the way.

"Easy there, friend."

While Kevin had been looking at where Luna lay, Ted, of all people, had gotten up onto the stage, and he had a gun held expertly in both hands.

"If you put the weapon down, we can talk about this," he said.

The man behind Kevin didn't move the knife from his throat. "It's talking that's the problem. He's talking to them. He's bringing them here to kill us! No, stay back!"

He punctuated that order by pointing the knife at Ted's advancing form. With the knife gone from his throat for a moment, Kevin did the only thing he could think off, and let himself fall to the floor.

Two shots rang out, so loud they seemed deafening. Kevin heard something metallic clatter to the stage, and something soft followed it a moment later. An instant after that, and Ted was there, pulling him to his feet.

"Don't look around. There are things a kid shouldn't have to see. Run to the others."

Kevin wanted to do all of that. He wanted to run and see if Luna was all right. He wanted to run to his mother, who was, even now, pushing her way through the chaos. He wanted to do all of that, but he couldn't, for one simple reason.

"There's a signal coming!" he said.

CHAPTER ELEVEN

Kevin could feel the next message coming, the signal starting in his headphones, the beginnings of a translation working their way up through him. This was happening now, whether he wanted it or not.

"I don't think we have much time," he said. "I can feel it coming."

Already, people were crowding around him. His mother was there, wrapping her arms around him as if she might protect him from anything that came. Dr. Levin and Professor Brewster were there, both looking worried. To Kevin's relief, Luna was back up on her feet. She hadn't been stabbed. Kevin ran to her, hugging her.

"Are you all right?" he asked.

"That depends," she said. "How many of you are there supposed to be?"

Kevin shook his head. "Don't joke, I was worried about you."

"*You* were worried about *me*? I wasn't the one with a knife to my throat."

Through it all, of course, the cameras kept rolling. They weren't going to stop in the middle of something this dramatic.

Professor Brewster was there, looking as though he was afraid Kevin might break. Or maybe it was just that he was staring at the dead man behind Kevin, the one that he didn't dare turn to face.

"What's happening?" he demanded. "Why are we not getting Kevin out of here?"

"He says there's another message coming," Ted explained.

Kevin didn't know how to explain it any clearer than that.

"Well, hold it back until we get you to safety," Professor Brewster said, but surely he had to know that it didn't work like that by now.

Kevin gritted his teeth. "I can't control when the message arrives. I just receive it and translate it."

"Why… why is it a problem if you get the message here?" Luna asked. She sounded shaky, which was understandable given everything the two of them had just been through. Even so, she was the one asking the right questions, not the professor.

"Because it will be the coordinates for the escape capsules," Kevin said. "I'm sure of it. What else could it be?"

"You remembered the numbers for the system before," Luna pointed out. "You could remember this."

"What if it's a long list?" Kevin countered. "What if I miss something?"

Luna pointed to the cameras, and Kevin realized she had a point. All he had to do was speak, and everything he said would be recorded by so many cameras he couldn't count them all. It would be around the world in an instant.

He went over to them, and even as he did it, the signal hit him.

The strings of numbers seemed to last forever. No wonder the beings sending them had given Kevin a warning that they would be coming. They'd wanted to give him a chance to prepare to record them in some way, so that the information wouldn't be lost. Each time Kevin finished repeating a string of numbers, a new string of digits and symbols began, barely giving him enough time to take a breath. He was translating it as it came, shaking with the effort of doing it, or perhaps just with the aftereffects of everything he'd been through in the past few minutes.

He recited the numbers and letters in a long, almost endless string, but the truth was that, for the first time since Luna had helped him to work out the connection to the Trappist system, he didn't know exactly what any of it meant.

Finally, the stream of numbers came to a stop, and Kevin stood there, trying to catch his breath.

"Is that everything?" Luna asked. "Kevin, are you all right?"

Kevin managed to nod, although even that was an effort right then. He wasn't sure which part he was nodding for.

Dr. Levin was there then, putting an arm around each of them.

"Okay," Dr. Levin said, "let's get you both back inside. After everything that has happened, my guess is that a lot of people will want to talk to both of you, but I want to get you both checked out first and make sure that you're all right. I don't like how close you both came to being hurt back there."

As they turned to go, Kevin could hear the shouts from the gathered crowd as they started to come out of whatever stunned silence they'd been caught up in.

"Kevin, when are the aliens coming for us?" one man yelled.

"Kevin, what does life *mean*?"

"When are you going to admit this is a hoax?"

"Are you hurt?"

There were so many different questions being shouted at once that for a moment or two, Kevin wanted to just walk away and leave them to it. He didn't, though. He felt as though he had to say something, and this time it didn't have anything to do with the pressures of alien signals.

"I know a lot of you are looking to me for answers, but the truth is that I don't have many," Kevin said. "I'm just a kid. I don't have any special understanding. I don't even know why I'm the one who receives the messages that the aliens are sending."

"What happened today?" a reporter asked. "Why all these numbers? What is it about?"

Kevin inclined his head, trying to work out how much he was allowed to say. Then he realized that was probably the wrong way of thinking about it. Misunderstanding this had caused this. Someone had tried to kill him today, because they didn't understand the information he had. Because, given the space to do it, they jumped to the wrong conclusion.

"Someone tried to kill me today," he said, "because they think the information I'm receiving is dangerous enough to be worth killing for."

"Is it?" someone called out.

Kevin shook his head. "Knowing that there's an alien civilization out there, that there *was* one, is amazing, but it's not worth killing people for, and I don't want anyone else being in danger for me." He almost stopped as he thought back to the sight of Luna being knocked aside, the sound of Ted's gun as he fired. "I don't matter. What matters is that the aliens' world was dying, and they have sent out... I guess you could call them time capsules. And we know where those are going now."

He also knew where he was going now, because his mother was pulling Kevin back away from the platform, into the institute.

***

"If my son is going to be attacked, then I don't want him staying here!" Kevin's mother said while she and Professor Brewster argued.

Kevin watched them both from the edge of his bed. He winced as one of the institute's medical staff disinfected a tiny cut he'd gotten from the knife. Beside him, Luna had a bandage wrapped around her head, while Ted was there, looking as though he was half expecting another attack.

"I understand your concern," Professor Brewster said, and even Kevin knew that was the wrong thing to say to his mother right then.

"You understand what it's like to see your child attacked because he's caught up in all something crazy?" Kevin's mother demanded. "Do you even have children?"

"Well no, but…"

"Who are you?" Kevin asked Ted, ignoring the argument between his mother and the professor for the moment.

"Oh, I'm just a guy who helps out where he can," Ted said.

"That's not an answer," Luna said.

He seemed to think for a moment or two, then shrugged. "I guess it can't hurt. Sorry, I'm just in the habit of not saying anything. I used to be in the army. Special Forces. Then I got loaned out to the CIA for a while, then… well, *then* I tried to retire, but I got a call when all of this started, and I couldn't exactly refuse."

"You said before that the President called you," Kevin said. "He wouldn't do that if you were just some guy."

"Well, maybe I've seen a few things in my time," Ted said. He looked over to where Professor Brewster and Kevin's mother were still arguing. "From what I hear, he *met* you about this though. That must make you more special than I am. You two want to come see how the eggheads are getting on with the numbers you pulled out of the air?"

Kevin nodded, and together, the three of them set off through the facility. Kevin felt a little stronger now, most of the weakness he'd felt obviously down to the combination of receiving the message and the stress of the attack. He also felt strangely empty, and it took him a moment to realize why:

For the first time since this had begun, there was no sense of the aliens.

There was no countdown pulsing in his head. There was no impending signal he was supposed to be waiting for. There were no messages. Everything was silent. It should have felt peaceful, but for the first time since he'd gotten there, Kevin felt… useless, as if he had nothing to do.

He was about the only one who did. The people they passed were busy, and they all seemed to be working on the problem of the coordinates. Labs that were used for other things stood empty, and instead, scientists were gathered in conference rooms, working on strings of numbers in a hundred different ways. Some of the NSA people seemed to be involved too.

Kevin had thought that there might be a problem with security as they got closer to the space that housed the supercomputers, but

Ted walked right through it all, soldiers and FBI agents alike nodding to him as he went and letting the three of them through.

"Wow," Luna said as they reached the supercomputer pit. "Imagine the games you could play on *those*."

Kevin doubted that they'd be much use for that, but when it came to dissecting strings of numbers, it seemed that they were *very* good. SAM was spitting out possibilities using the signals, while half of the other machines there had been fired up too, and scientists ran between them, calling out results.

"It's another miss," one yelled. "I think that one hits somewhere out in the Pleiades."

Kevin heard a groan of frustration from the other scientists there.

"They're trying to narrow down the search," Ted explained.

Dr. Levin was there, and to Kevin's surprise, people seemed to be listening to her. Maybe the fact that there were definitely aliens made it easier to take orders from the head of SETI.

"The problem is too much information," she said. "You gave us so many possible hits, Kevin, that we can't work through all of it, even with our computing power."

"Have you tried the Internet?" Kevin asked.

"I don't think this is the kind of thing we'd find on the Internet," Professor Brewster said, coming up to join them. "We have some of the most sophisticated computers in the world here."

Kevin shook his head. "We might. When I translated, I gave the reporters the information, right? So, won't people all around the world have been looking at it? You said the problem was having enough people to do it. Well, doesn't this mean you have the whole world helping?"

"The kid has a point," Ted said. "Have you checked?"

"Well... no," Professor Brewster admitted.

Dr. Levin shrugged. "Maybe it's worth a try. SETI has often borrowed computing power from people around the world."

"Do it," Ted said.

Dr. Levin went away for a few moments. She came back with a tablet computer, and a faintly shocked look.

"I... I don't believe it," she said, and started tapping away on it. "Hold on, I'll bring it up on a bigger screen."

She pressed a few points on the tablet, and a computer screen across from them lit up, big enough that the entire room would be able to see it. Coordinates sat on the screen, along with the words "Alien craft to hit Earth!" The site appeared to be anonymous, but there was no doubt about what it was saying.

"If we take this set of coordinates," Dr. Levin said, "well, watch."

A map of the world appeared on the screen, first so broad that Kevin couldn't work out where the crash site was supposed to be. It turned, zooming in on South America, then kept going. It took in a country, then a region, then what seemed like a patch of jungle just a couple of miles across.

"The Colombian rainforest," Ted said, staring at it.

"We're sure about this?" Professor Brewster asked.

"We'll check, of course," Dr. Levin said, "but on first glance... yes, it looks correct. Which is astonishing in its own way. The idea that a civilization could predict where their vessel would land this precisely at such a distance is... almost impossible to believe."

"Well, I think we need to start believing it." Ted put a hand on Kevin's shoulder. "If you're right about all this, our alien friends are sending their cargo to Colombia."

"Is that a bad thing?" Kevin asked.

Ted shrugged. "I don't know. It might make things complicated. I'm more worried about how many other people will have seen this. Dr. Levin?"

"There's no way to know," the SETI director said. "I'd guess that if we found it, plenty of other people will have."

"Which means that half the world will be there," Ted said. "What do you say we go there to meet them, Kevin?"

"Go to meet who?" Kevin's mother asked, walking into the computer pit. "What's going on?"

Kevin tried to work out the best way to phrase it. "Mom, um... can I go to Colombia?"

CHAPTER TWELVE

"You don't need to come, Mom," Kevin said as he and the others found themselves waved through security at the San Francisco airport. She was just a step away from him, as if afraid that moving further would mean losing him in the chaos of the airport. Ted was close by too, although Kevin suspected it was for different reasons.

"Of course I need to come," his mother said, wheeling along a small suitcase that made it look as though she'd packed for a vacation. "One moment people are trying to murder you, and the next, you're flying off to the middle of a jungle? Do you think I'm going to let you do that alone?"

"I wouldn't be *alone*, Mom," Kevin pointed out. If anything, it seemed like the entire institute was heading to Colombia, packing itself aboard not one but two chartered airplanes, and taking with it an array of equipment designed to search for the escape capsule.

"I'm still coming," his mother said, and Kevin knew better than to argue with that tone.

One person who wasn't coming was Luna, and Kevin found that he was already missing having her there. She'd gone home, because *her* parents apparently had stricter views about her flying to South America in search of aliens.

Professor Brewster stood toward the front, marshalling the scientists and the soldiers, the agents and the occasional reporters as they loaded onto the plane.

"Are you all set, Kevin?" he asked. "We have a long flight ahead of us."

Kevin nodded. "I can't believe we're doing this."

"We nearly aren't," Professor Brewster said. "A lot of people are having to pull a lot of strings to let us fly into Colombia for this. Now, hurry and get aboard."

Kevin got onto the plane and found a seat where he could look out of the window. His mother took one next to him, while Ted took one just in front of him.

"It's a long way to Colombia," Ted said. "It's been a while."

"You were there before?" Kevin asked.

"Officially?" he said with a faint smile. "Never been there in my life."

"And unofficially?" Kevin asked.

82

"Oh, it was very unofficial the last time I was there," Ted replied. "Things are a bit more peaceful there now though. There are still a few cartels, but without the civil war going on, the government can pay a bit more attention to them."

"It sounds cool," Kevin said.

His mother didn't agree. "It sounds like a dangerous place to take my son."

"I'm sure it will be fine," Ted said. Kevin heard the doors to the plane shutting as the last people climbed aboard. "Besides, it's too late to turn back now. Nine hours from now, and we'll be in Bogota."

Nine hours. How did you spend nine hours cooped up in a confined space with a bunch of scientists? It seemed to Kevin that practically everyone there was having to find the answer to that question. Some played games on phones, or read, or watched movies. Kevin's mother mostly slept. Kevin alternated looking out of the window with trying to get some rest and occasionally putting on the headphones with the signal stream, just in case there was anything to hear. There wasn't.

"I don't even know if these will work so far from the research institute," Kevin said, after the third time he'd done it.

"I asked the scientists that before we left," Ted said. "They've set it up so the base signal is relayed over the Internet. Anywhere you have a connection, you can access the signal."

Kevin supposed he shouldn't have been surprised by that. Of course they would want to make sure that he could hear it, whatever happened. They wouldn't want to risk missing an important message. Even so, the idea of being able to listen in from anywhere in the world seemed impressive.

Kevin spent some of the time looking down at the places they passed over. He'd never even been out of state before, yet here he was flying over deserts and thick rainforests, cities and patches of ocean. He thought about the people down there. Did they know about the escape capsule? What did they think about the possibility of actually finding alien life?

He got part of an answer when they landed in Bogota. He immediately saw a dozen similar groups, all carrying equipment that looked suspiciously similar to the gear they'd brought with them.

"Looks as though we weren't the only ones who worked out where those coordinates led," Ted said as he looked over the collection of them. He seemed fairly relaxed about it, but Professor Brewster was anything but calm.

"This is simply *unacceptable*," the scientist said. "The Swiss are here, and that looks like a group from the private tech sector, and those are the *Canadians*. After all the effort we've put into uncovering this information, I can't believe that they're planning to snatch the capsule from under us."

Kevin wanted to say that they didn't know for sure that was what the other groups were there for, but he couldn't think of another reason they might be there. He wasn't sure how he felt about their presence.

On the one hand, he wanted to believe that the aliens' message was intended for the whole of humanity, and that it should be shared. He was happy that he'd had to shout the coordinates to the news cameras or risk losing them for that reason. At the same time, Professor Brewster was kind of right: Kevin was the one who had been able to translate the alien signal, not the others, and he wanted to at least *see* the escape capsule now that he had.

"We'll just have to be the first to it," Professor Brewster said, although Kevin suspected that it was going to be easier said than done. He couldn't see how they were going to get through the airport any quicker than the others, or get to the jungle quicker, or even search quicker.

They tried, though. Kevin would have laughed at the sight of a dozen sets of scientists conducting a strange kind of race through the Bogota airport, except that he had to keep up with them all, trying to find gaps in the press of people and making sure that he didn't lose sight of his mother at the same time.

"This way!" Professor Brewster called, leading the way toward what looked like a rental car desk. "Hello, we need to rent... let's see, probably a dozen off-road vehicles and a small truck."

"I'm sorry," the woman at the desk said. "As I told the last gentleman to ask for that, it is simply not something that we keep here at the airport. Most people... well, they do not need this for their vacation, you see?"

"This is not a *vacation*," Professor Brewster declared. "This is a scientific expedition of the utmost importance!"

"Even so."

Dr. Levin stepped in. "Come on, David, you know we'll need to rest first, and then we can work on the actual expedition after that."

"And meanwhile the Canadians will be getting ahead of us!" he complained. "How did they even get here so fast?"

There didn't seem to be an answer to that, but Kevin found himself swept up as they made their way from the airport to the spot where the American embassy stood waiting, looking like a large gray block in the middle of Bogota.

The ambassador was waiting for them within. He shook Professor Brewster's hand, and then shook Kevin's, much to his surprise.

"I got the call that you were coming from the President a couple of hours ago. It will be a little cramped with so many of you here, but I've had rooms prepared for you all, and I'm working to arrange transport for your team to the rainforest. You should be aware that the Colombian government isn't entirely happy about this, but we're working to smooth the way for you."

It didn't sound good that the government of the country where they were looking didn't like them being there. By that point, Kevin was too tired to worry about it. He fell asleep almost as soon as the embassy staff showed him to a room, and didn't wake up again until he heard Professor Brewster's voice shouting from outside.

"Come on, everyone! The embassy has managed to get us some transport, and we need to be ready to go before everyone else beats us to the prize!"

Kevin did his best to get ready in a hurry. Even so, by the time he got out there, most of the others were already ready. Professor Brewster had acquired a khaki shirt and trousers that made him look the way someone might think an explorer looked if they'd only ever seen pictures of them. His mother was wearing her normal clothes, augmented by a wide sun hat. Ted just looked like Ted.

"Quickly," Professor Brewster said, clapping his hands. "Quickly! We can't allow anyone else any more of a head start."

He hurried off, trying to get everyone out of the hotel.

"*Will* everyone else already be at the capsule?" Kevin asked Ted. Professor Brewster might be in charge of the expedition, but Ted was the one who knew what he was doing. Half of the people there already seemed to be looking to him to find out what to do.

The former soldier shook his head. "I doubt it. The rainforest at night is tricky. It's easy to get turned around, even without the wildlife. The sensible move was for everyone to stay put overnight, then move this morning."

Kevin guessed it was also the move they'd all made, at least if the sold out hotels were anything to go by. There must be people from all around the world trying to find the escape pod, and all because of the numbers he'd managed to translate.

"Well, kid," Ted said. "You've brought us this far. I guess it's time to find out what's at the end of all of it."

85

They went downstairs, to where it turned out that the embassy had managed to find them trucks and SUVs, a couple of old Jeeps, and a few older cars.

"Just stay close," Ted said, as he picked out a Jeep and jumped into the driver's seat.

They drove, sticking together in a convoy that snaked back at the speed of the slowest car, which was, Kevin thought, pretty slow. A part of him didn't mind that too much, because Colombia was beautiful. More of him wanted to curse the slow vehicles and the increasingly pitted roads, because he wanted to see the vessel the aliens had used to carry themselves. He wanted to see the outcome of everything he'd done.

They kept going, and as they got nearer to the area of rainforest the coordinates pointed to, the roads got worse. Then, as trees started to hem the road in on either side, they were blocked entirely by traffic, and it took Kevin a few moments to realize what was going on.

A truck lay on its side in the middle of the road, another having dents in it big enough to suggest a collision. There were more trucks and cars all around, with people standing there waiting, or trying to work out what to do, or arguing in a dozen languages. Kevin recognized some of the people there, and he knew who they had to be.

"Aren't they the other research groups?" Kevin asked, as they pulled up. He saw Ted nod, but before the former soldier could say anything, Professor Brewster was there, moving up from another vehicle.

"Why are we stopped?" he asked.

"You can see why," Ted said.

"But can't we just drive around them?" Professor Brewster asked.

Ted gestured to the trees that grew close by either side of the road. "If you can do it, be my guest."

Professor Brewster looked as though he might say something, then shook his head and set off to join the argument.

"Do you think it will make any difference?" Kevin's mother asked.

Ted shrugged.

Ahead, Professor Brewster started arguing with half a dozen other people, some pointing fingers as they tried to work out exactly who was responsible for dealing with the problems there. Since Kevin couldn't imagine the research institute's director settling for talking to someone who wasn't in charge, he guessed that the other people there arguing on the muddy road must be directors of their own organizations. Sometimes adults made no sense.

He jumped down from the Jeep, as much because he wanted to see what was going on as because he actually thought he could help. He walked forward to where two or three people were arguing over a winch, while a crowd of bored-looking scientists and soldiers looked on.

"If you have a winch, why isn't anyone using it?" he asked.

A man with a thick Scandinavian accent answered. "Because it is our winch, and our director doesn't want us helping others to get to the... object first."

"But that's stupid," Kevin said.

"Kevin," his mother said, catching up. "All of these people are very clever. They probably all have PhDs."

"They're still being stupid," Kevin said, and he was surprised to find them looking at him rather than just ignoring him. They knew who he was, he realized, and they seemed to be looking at him as if waiting for him to decide what to do.

"Why don't you just work together?" he asked.

"I told you," the man who'd spoken before said. "We can't let them use our winch until—"

"Not the winch," Kevin said. "The whole thing. The aliens sent their escape capsule to this planet, not to one country, so why don't we work together to find it?"

"And see it taken back to America?" one of those there asked.

"Well, we could find somewhere else," Kevin suggested. "Somewhere we could all look at it."

The men were quiet for a few moments as they started to think. One took out a map.

"There's a UN facility a few miles from Bogota," he said.

Another nodded. "I've done some work there on newly discovered plants. It has good facilities."

"Our bosses might still want to argue," the first said, a little uncertainly.

Kevin had an answer to that. "Then *they* can argue while *we're* all opening the alien escape capsule."

When he put it like that, the others didn't seem to want to argue anymore. Instead, they started to connect up the winch, the researchers who had been standing around moving in to shift the truck from where it had toppled.

"Well done," Ted said as Kevin returned to him. "Not many people could have talked them into working together."

Kevin shrugged. It had seemed like the obvious thing to do.

"What is all this?" Professor Brewster asked. "What's going on? Why are they moving again?"

"We're going to go find the escape capsule together," Kevin's mother explained.

"But no one authorized that," Professor Brewster said. "I didn't authorize that."

"But it means that we're moving," Kevin's mother said. "Is it so wrong that we're working together?"

"No," Professor Brewster said. Kevin guessed that he was just a bit surprised not to be the one making the decisions for once. "I suppose not. But this doesn't mean that I trust them. When it comes to the cut and thrust of academic debate, I wouldn't trust those Canadians as far as I could throw them. Be on your guard, all of you."

He walked off, calling out orders to their people, and to some of the other groups as well. Kevin wondered if anyone was paying attention. He looked over to Ted.

"*Should* we be suspicious of the others?" he asked.

The former soldier shrugged. "Maybe, maybe not. Sometimes you work with people and you don't know what they're going to do down the road. For the moment, only one thing matters."

"We're going to find the capsule," Kevin said.

Ted nodded. "We're going to find the capsule."

CHAPTER THIRTEEN

Kevin had never been in a jungle before, but it was nothing like he'd seen on TV. There, jungles were just a few palm leaves in the background, with plenty of space for people to run and fight, and they moved quickly. In the real thing, plant life pressed in on all sides, with only a few tracks worn by animals, and soldiers having to hack a route for them as they got deeper into it.

They didn't show the rain either. That came down as they walked, steadily soaking their whole party in bursts that seemed to fill the whole world beneath the canopy.

"Is it always like this?" Professor Brewster called out.

One of the guides shrugged. "It is called a *rain*forest for a reason, sir."

Kevin wasn't sure how quickly they were moving, but it didn't *feel* that quick. He'd assumed that, as ill as he was, he wouldn't be able to keep up with the rest. Instead, he trekked along with them, the slowest of the scientists moving far slower than he did. Maybe it didn't help that half of them wanted to stop every few hundred yards to take samples of insect life or unusual plants.

"They can't help themselves," Ted said. He kept pace with Kevin, never more than a few yards from his side, as if afraid that going further would mean losing him in the jungle. "Cleverest people you'll ever meet, but it just means that a place like this is too full of potential discoveries. They think about being the one who spots a new species of butterfly, or finds a substance that will cure cancer, and they forget about how big the thing we're here to do is. All they can think about is how full of life the jungle is."

Kevin couldn't blame them, because the jungle *was* full of life, in a way he couldn't have believed. It seemed that everywhere he looked, there were plants he hadn't seen before, from the giant trees that formed a canopy to the creepers that wound their way between them and the lower level things that snatched what light they could on the jungle floor. There were insects and lizards, small mammals and occasional rustles in the brush that suggested bigger things.

Oh, and spiders, big enough that Kevin didn't want to go anywhere near them. The only fun part of that was that it seemed Professor Brewster was particularly afraid of them, jumping so high every time he saw one that Kevin thought he might reach the canopy.

"What do you think about when you're here?" Kevin asked Ted.

"Aside from the mission?" The soldier shrugged. "Mostly memories of the last time I was here. You need to be careful, Kevin."

"I'm not going to wander off," Kevin said. Sometimes people treated him like he wasn't thirteen. Like he was just... a child or something.

"Not what I meant," Ted said. "Things are better after the peace with FARC, but there are still cartels out there who don't like people coming into their territory. Even the army. A collection of different scientific groups? We'd be easy prey for the wrong people."

He shot a look to where a group of soldiers from half a dozen different nations were helping to clear the way, hacking their way through with the certainty of people who'd had to do it many times before in other places.

"It's not just that, is it?" Kevin asked. "You don't trust the people we're working with."

"After they've spent the last day racing to be the first one there?" Ted shook his head. "But that's common enough. We're all going for something valuable. We *have* a valuable asset, in you, because you can translate the signals. Maybe nothing will happen. Maybe this will all go fine, but you know what they say: hope for the best, prepare for the worst."

Put like that, the jungle seemed a more threatening place than it had before, full of spots where it might be easy to reach out and grab someone. Kevin did his best to ignore it.

One thing he couldn't ignore was the heat. He'd thought that, since he was from California, the difference wouldn't be too much, just a few degrees hotter, at most. He hadn't thought about the effects of the rain, which combined with the heat to turn the whole place into a kind of giant pressure cooker, steam visibly coming off people as they walked.

"Are you doing okay, Kevin?" Dr. Levin asked.

He nodded. "I'm fine."

"You'll tell someone if you aren't?" she asked. She looked over to where Kevin's mother was making her way along the track behind them. "Your mother is pretty worried that we're doing the wrong thing, bringing you here."

"I want to be here," Kevin said. He knew that the scientist was just trying to look out for him, but he wanted to see this. He wanted

90

to find the object that the aliens had sent to Earth. He wanted to see where everything he'd translated led.

"Well, I just hope it isn't too much further," Dr. Levin said. "You might be fine, but I'm melting in this heat."

"Not much further to the spot we saw," Ted said, checking a robust-looking GPS readout. "Just a little more that way."

They kept going, finding a clearing to use as a base while they searched. Some of the soldiers started to set up rough awnings to keep the rain off, while the different groups of scientists set up equipment that they had carried through the jungle. They brought out what looked like metal detectors and strange devices that fit onto small carts that could be pulled by hand. Some set up enough computing equipment that they could probably have run their usual labs from there if they hadn't been so cut off from the world. The strangest part of it was watching half a dozen sets of nearly identical equipment dragged out

"The object that came to Earth fell somewhere in this vicinity," Professor Brewster said, obviously assuming that he was in charge. "We need to find it. That means that we spread out and locate the general area of a crash site by looking for damage, then use our equipment to locate the object."

"Stay safe," Ted said, and Kevin suspected that if he didn't say it, no one would have. Professor Brewster would happily have sent people off into the jungle with no more direction than that. "Always work in pairs, so that if anything happens, the other one can get help. Stay close to camp, and stay in contact. The jungle *will* try to get you lost. Watch out for the wildlife, and don't go into any watercourses. There are caiman and snakes in this area."

The scientists moved out cautiously, accompanied by soldiers and whatever local guides they'd been able to find.

"Do we go and look?" Kevin asked.

Ted shook his head. "It's better to wait for now. Let other people do the work of finding it. You'll see it soon enough. Now, I'd better go make a phone call."

He got up, taking out a satellite phone that would probably work now that they were in the clearing, with a clear path to the sky. He walked a little way away, talking quietly. Kevin thought about creeping closer to hear what he was saying, but something about the way the soldier was talking suggested that it might not be a good idea.

"I think we've found something!" one of the scientists called out, from within the jungle.

Kevin couldn't sit there, and neither, it seemed, could any of the others in the small camp. He found himself just one of those rushing forward, hurrying to keep up through the jungle, the soft earth underneath giving way as his feet pushed into it. He followed the scientists into another small clearing. Kevin had been half expecting a crater there, surrounded by desolation. Instead, there were just a few scars on the earth, hinting at something coming through there.

The strange part was that the trees around it didn't seem to be damaged. If something had fallen to Earth in the recent past, shouldn't there have been damage, wreckage, even smoldering embers?

Then Kevin realized that he was thinking about it the wrong way. The aliens had sent their messages years ago, even traveling at the speed of light. Why would their escape capsule have only just arrived? Why wouldn't it have been here years, even decades, waiting for someone to discover it? He found that he liked that idea, of something secret waiting there for him to uncover it. It made him feel like a treasure hunter.

The scientists had already started to work their way along it, working with their various devices. From what Kevin could hear, he didn't think it was going very well.

"I'm not getting any responses from the metal detector," Phil called. The researcher had sweated clean through his Hawaiian shirt by now. "I haven't heard it this quiet… well, *ever*."

"I'm not getting any response looking for a heat signature," another of them called out.

"Well, we wouldn't," Phil called back. "It's been cooling all the time since it landed, and we don't know when that was. What about the magnetometer?"

A scientist dragging the thing that had looked like a handcart shook his head. "The ground's too uneven. I can't tell if I'm getting signals or just interference."

Apparently, the ground-penetrating radar had the same problem, although Kevin hadn't known before then that such a thing existed. He didn't really know how half of the scientists' equipment worked; it could have been magic, although he doubted they would have liked that comparison. From where he was standing, it just meant watching a bunch of scientists run about with devices and wires, watching screens or listening to things beep. It was fun to watch, for maybe the first hour.

"We will just have to dig," Professor Brewster said eventually. "It must be here somewhere, so if we dig up all of it, eventually we will find it."

It seemed that "we" in this case didn't include Professor Brewster, because the institute's director made no move to pick up a shovel. Plenty of scientists did, though, and even a few soldiers helped, attacking the earth around them as if it might reveal its secrets if they just worked hard enough.

There didn't seem to be anything for Kevin to do except wait. He didn't have a shovel, and in any case it didn't seem like the best way to find anything. It was just digging randomly in the hope that something would happen. It seemed a bit like digging random holes on a beach in the hope that one would contain a pirate chest. He stood there instead, trying to keep out of their way as they dug.

That was when he felt the whisper of connection through the trees, almost indefinable. It felt a little like the pulse of the countdown within him, except that this pulsing seemed to get stronger as he took a few steps along the path the falling escape capsule must have taken. When he stepped the other way, it grew weaker.

Kevin stopped, trying to be certain. He didn't want to say that he knew what he was doing until he was sure it was more than just some random feeling inside him. What if it was just the heat?

"It isn't," Kevin told himself, wishing he were as certain as he tried to sound.

Kevin started forward, trying to follow that pulsing, staying with it as it grew stronger, picking his way between the trees. Every time it got weaker again, he stopped, walking around in a circle until he found the direction that felt strongest. It wasn't long before he had a clear route, which brought him out onto what looked like a small deer track. Kevin followed it along until he reached a space where it opened out to reveal a large natural pool, as wide across as a swimming pool, its water green-brown. Instinctively, Kevin knew that the object that had come to Earth was there somewhere, beneath the surface. He could feel its pull so strongly now that he took a step toward the pool, then another, trying to remember the reason why he'd been told he shouldn't do exactly that...

A scaled shape came up out of the water, teeth snapping in a lunge that sent Kevin backpedaling, barely fast enough to avoid it. He would have thought of alligators if Ted hadn't given them all a warning earlier. This creature's snout was too long and pointed, its shape a bit too sleek. The caiman kept coming, moving out of the water low to the ground, its tail dragging an S-shaped track behind it.

"Help!" Kevin called. He wanted to turn and run, but he guessed that the moment he tried to, the thing would be on him. Instead, he continued to back away, while the caiman advanced with a growl that promised that Kevin would be its next meal. Kevin felt the press of a tree against his back and knew that he'd missed the trail, which meant that the caiman was gaining ground. It opened its jaws, showing what seemed like endless teeth—

The roar of gunfire came, so loud against the jungle that Kevin thought he might go deaf. The caiman made a hissing sound of pain, then slumped. Kevin slumped too, only the tree holding him upright as Ted moved into view with a rifle raised to his shoulder. He only lowered it once he seemed certain the beast was dead.

"Are you okay?" he asked.

Kevin managed to nod, in spite of the fear that still gripped him. "I think so."

"What were you doing? I thought I told you not to wander off."

Kevin wanted to say that he wasn't a little kid. Instead, he nodded to the pool of dark water. "I had to, I sensed… I think that it's in there."

He saw the soldier blink, then look toward the water. "You're sure?"

"Yes," Kevin said. "I don't know *how* I'm sure, but it's there."

To his surprise, Ted didn't question that any further, just called for the others. They came, in just as much of a hurry as when they'd found the initial signs of damage. They weren't quite as quick to plunge into the water, though, obviously afraid of what might still lurk there. Eventually, Ted and three other soldiers, two Scandinavian and one American, stepped into it, wading around with a tarpaulin for a net.

"We have something," Ted called back, and they wrapped it around the thing, hauling together to lift it, dragging it from the water. It seemed to take forever, and Kevin found himself expecting something huge as they worked to pull it out, a dozen of the scientists moving to help them.

When it finally rolled out from the tarpaulin onto the ground, it wasn't what Kevin expected at all. He'd been thinking it would be bigger, for one thing. His imagination had told him that there would be a vehicle bigger than a car, maybe close to the size of a house. He'd thought it would be silver and shining, or so black that it looked like the space through which it had flown.

Instead, a perfectly round sphere of rock sat there, still slimy with the water, but smooth beneath. It looked as though someone had fired a rocky bowling ball across the universe, or perhaps shot it out of some great cannon toward the Earth.

Even so, the scientists clustered around it until Kevin could barely see it because they were so many of them.

"Is this it?" Professor Brewster asked. "Let me through, let me through. Have we found it?"

"We found something, definitely," Dr. Levin said. She sounded as though she was trying to force herself to stay calm, not get too excited. "Now we just have to work out exactly what."

Ted was shaking his head. "Before we do any of that, there's at least one other thing that we need to do. We need to get it back."

CHAPTER FOURTEEN

Kevin didn't want to take his eyes off the rock while they carried it back on a kind of stretcher, not entirely sure what to make of it as they walked it back through the jungle to their base camp. He was both excited and puzzled, caught between the joy at having found what the alien signals had pointed them toward and the surprise of it not being the great silvery spaceship that he'd imagined it might be.

It felt weird, having actually found it, even though they'd all come here to do exactly that. It felt as though it shouldn't be there, but it was, and now Kevin could barely contain his excitement at the possibility of seeing what lay inside.

"We'll open it up when we get it back, right?" he asked Dr. Levin, who seemed to be looking on with the air of someone waiting for Christmas.

Beside him, Dr. Levin nodded. "That's the idea. There will be a lab waiting for us at the UN compound outside Bogota, and we'll see what's inside."

He could hear her trying not to get too excited by it all. In fact, most of the scientists there seemed to be just as happy to have found this strangely smooth rock as they would have been if they'd found some kind of intact alien spaceship, bristling with advanced technology. Maybe it was just that they were scientists, and a rock seemed more *real* somehow to them. They were probably used to testing rocks from outer space, being from NASA, while spaceships seemed impossible to them.

Even so, Kevin was hoping that things would be a lot cooler once they opened it up. Maybe there would be alien technology inside, or messages left in it like a message in a bottle. Unless the aliens were really tiny, he doubted that there were any in there, but maybe they were that small, or they'd found a way to fit more into spaces than they should hold, or something.

Whatever it was, it would be amazing.

They walked back to the space where they'd left the trucks, and already, there were scientists there packing away their gear. It seemed as though they were as eager to get back and open up the rock they'd recovered as Kevin was. When they were getting the equipment out they'd been delicate with it, but now they practically threw it into the back of the vehicles.

"We should get into the trucks," Dr. Levin said. "We're almost ready to go, I think."

Kevin nodded, starting to go back to the Jeep. He saw Professor Brewster along the way, and was going to run around him, but to Kevin's surprise, the NASA institute's head actually looked happy. He was practically dancing in place with excitement.

"We found it," Professor Brewster said. "We actually found it. This is... I know I've been hard on you, Kevin, but it was only because I wanted to be certain of this. Ever since I was... well, since I was your age."

Kevin could hardly believe it; he had never expected Professor Brewster, of all people, to have a childlike optimism.

He ran back to the Jeep where Ted and his mom waited. For possibly the first time since this had begun, his mother had the kind of wonder on her face that told Kevin she finally understood this, that she wasn't just doing it for Kevin's sake. Ted seemed a bit less obviously happy. If Ted was worried about something, that couldn't be good. After all, he'd faced down a caiman with no problems.

It couldn't dent Kevin's happiness, though. All the scientists had come in with their testing machines, and he'd been the one to pick out the spot where the alien capsule sat. It felt as though it was his somehow because of that, even while it sat in a truck twenty yards away, guarded by a mixture of scientists and soldiers of different nations. It felt as though whatever happened from now on, it would be down to him.

"What do you think will be inside the capsule once we open it up?" Kevin asked.

Ted thought about it for a few seconds

"They could have sent a time capsule full of information. Maybe they're hoping that someone out there has the technology to bring them back from what happened to them. You'd have to ask the scientists. They'd know more."

Maybe they would. At the very least, most of them seemed to be talking about it, so that the convoy's radios seemed alive with speculation in different languages. Kevin hadn't heard them as excited as that since the messages began. Maybe it was the part where they had something more than a signal translated by a thirteen-year-old boy. Maybe they liked having something solid to prove what was happening.

Kevin couldn't blame them for that. Even though he'd known that what he was seeing was real, finding the rock had been a kind of relief. It had been proof of just how much all this meant.

"How long until we're at the UN compound?" Kevin asked. He just wanted to get there now, so that they could get on with looking.

"That depends," Ted said. "We've already seen how tricky the roads can—damn it."

For a moment, Kevin thought there must be another blockage across the road. Then he saw the ribbon of uniformed figures there holding guns.

He stared at them in shock. Kevin could hear the chatter of the others on the radio as they saw what was happening. Even Ted seemed tense. Although not surprised. He looked, if anything, as though he'd been expecting this.

"Too late to reverse," Ted said, slowing the Jeep. "There's too many people behind us. Looks like we'll have to do this the hard way."

He brought the vehicle to a halt, turning to Kevin. "They look like Colombian military rather than one of the cartels, so this should be okay, but if it isn't, stay here and keep your heads down. Understood?"

"Yes," Kevin's mother said.

Ted looked to Kevin. "Understood?"

"Okay," Kevin said. What did the former soldier think he was going to do? "Um… they aren't going to shoot us, are they?"

"Probably not," Ted said.

"*Probably* not?" That didn't sound very reassuring. Kevin would have preferred "definitely not" or even "don't worry about it."

Ted nodded to where Professor Brewster was already making his way to the front of the convoy. "I suspect it depends on who we let do the talking."

He jumped down, and Kevin could see a bunch of other figures moving past too, either eager to help, or wanting to show that they had some kind of authority there, or maybe just wanting to see what was happening.

That was certainly the reason he started to get out of the Jeep.

"Kevin," his mother said. "Ted told us to stay in the vehicle."

"I know, Mom," he said, "but I don't think it will make a lot of difference if there's some kind of fight."

"Kevin!" his mother said again, as Kevin hopped down from the Jeep and started forward. He heard his mother following after him, but he kept going. He wasn't going to miss this.

By the time he reached the group of armed figures, they were already discussing things in a tone that sounded dangerously close to violence. Kevin had seen kids at school when they'd gone past insulting one another, and they didn't want to back down because they thought it would make them look stupid. They always had that sense that they didn't want to fight, that they were scared and the whole thing was stupid, but they were going to anyway. Kevin had never expected to hear adults sounding like that, but at least some of them did.

"...And I am telling you, Professor, that this is *Colombia's* sovereign territory," an older man was saying to Professor Brewster. "If this artifact had fallen on US territory, are you telling me that you would permit us to take it away as you are trying to?"

"No, of course not, General," Professor Brewster snapped back. "Because *we* have the finest scientific facilities in the world."

"Are you impugning the quality of Colombia's scientific program?" the general asked.

"I'm saying that it doesn't have a tenth of the resources that we do," Professor Brewster replied.

That didn't seem to impress the other man. If anything, it only seemed to annoy him.

"So that's it, is it? The USA is the biggest and richest, and so we must all bow to what it wants?" Kevin saw him shake his head. "We've had enough of that in the past. You think I don't recognize some of the men here from the past?"

"When we were *invited*," Ted said, moving up to them. "General Marquez, I didn't hear you complaining when we were here helping your country against the cartels."

"And now you are helping yourselves," the other man said.

"We made contact through diplomatic channels," Professor Brewster said. "We told you that we would be coming."

"But you did not wait for *permission*," General Marquez said. Kevin had the feeling all of this was heading downhill fast, and he was caught in the middle of it with adults arguing around him. Adults who definitely wouldn't listen to someone like him, and who seemed to be determined to argue and shout until it all turned into violence.

"If you'll give me a minute, sir," Ted said, "I'm sure I can get our president on the phone for you, and yours."

"So that they can agree that we should do what you want in return for some minor concession, some empty promise?" the general demanded. "Our president is a good man, but this is a military matter."

"It's looking like it might become one," Ted said. The strange thing to Kevin was that he didn't raise his voice, even in the middle of a dangerous situation like that. Professor Brewster was sweating, and Kevin could feel his own nerves rising, but it seemed that the former soldier was just... calm.

It was a dangerous kind of calm, though, and it worried Kevin almost as much as the rest of it.

"I will make this simple," General Marquez said. "The artifact you are transporting belongs to the Colombian people. We will be taking possession of it. If you attempt to stop us from doing so, you will be arrested and imprisoned. Now, step back."

He made a move toward the first of the trucks in the convoy, obviously intending to check it for signs of anything alien.

"I can't allow you to touch that truck, sir," Ted said, and now, somehow, there was a weapon in his hand, pointed directly at the Colombian general.

Instantly, there were more guns pointing than Kevin had seen in his life.

CHAPTER FIFTEEN

Kevin tried his best not to look scared as dozens of weapons pointed his way. It wasn't easy. Most of the Colombian ones seemed to be pointed at Ted, but since Kevin wasn't standing that far away, the distinction didn't make much difference to him. Soldiers on their side, meanwhile, had taken the opportunity to level their own weapons at the Colombians. What had been a one-sided thing had turned into a dangerous standoff in a matter of seconds.

"You're still outgunned," General Marquez said. "If you fire, you would all die."

Ted shrugged. "With respect, sir, you would die first."

He moved so that the general was between him and the other Colombians.

"You think I care about that?" General Marquez demanded. "Something like this is more important than you, more important than me, and I *still* have superior firepower."

"Then it's a good thing I called in air support," Ted said.

"You're bluffing,"

But Kevin could hear the sound of rotor blades in the distance, and it seemed that so could everyone else. It should have made him feel safe, but as far as he could see, it made the whole situation more dangerous. It just increased the number of people who might decide to open fire at the wrong moment.

Sure enough, a helicopter came up over the trees, looking angular and spiked with weapons. Kevin found himself thinking of the phone call Ted had put in earlier. He'd expected this to happen, or at least something like this. He looked up at it, then around at all the men with guns pointed at one another. Another few seconds, and there might be bullets flying everywhere.

So Kevin did the only thing he could do, and stepped between Ted and the general.

"Get out of the way, Kevin," Ted said.

"You should move," General Marquez agreed.

Kevin shook his head. "No."

"Kevin!" his mother yelled from further back, but a couple of the researchers caught her arms as she started forward. *"Get away from there!"*

Kevin didn't move. He looked from Ted to the Colombian general, staying between the two of them while above, the helicopter hovered in a constant threat.

"You're both being idiots," Kevin said. It wasn't how you were supposed to speak to adults, certainly not ones who were that heavily armed, but as far as Kevin could see, it was only the truth.

"You don't understand what's going on here, Kevin," Ted said.

"He is right," General Marquez agreed. "You do not understand the implications of this."

Why did adults always think that they were the only ones who understood things? Why did they think that kids like Kevin were stupid?

"You don't want a bunch of people from outside Colombia coming in to take what's yours, or to tell you what to do," Kevin said, "because you think it's like them saying that they're better than you. And *Ted* doesn't want to give up the capsule partly because he thinks that we've done most of the work of finding it, partly because he thinks it will make us look weak if we let it go, and partly because he has orders and he's the kind of person who will follow them no matter what. It's all stupid."

Ted cocked his head to one side. "Kevin's not entirely wrong. I do have orders."

"And I *don't* want to see Colombia insulted by having this artifact taken by the Americans," General Marquez said. "You have already interfered in our country too much."

"So you're both just being stubborn," Kevin said. It felt wrong, talking to the two adults like this, but it was just the truth, and anyway, if he didn't, they were probably all going to be shot. It seemed like a good reason to keep going, so he gestured to the scientists. "Look at all the different countries here working together. If they can do it, why don't you?"

"What do you suggest?" General Marquez asked.

Kevin had an answer for that, at least. "We were going to take the capsule to some UN place…"

"The WHO center there," Ted supplied.

"So why not do that?" Kevin asked. "It would look as though it was all happening because you allowed it, and you could be there when we opened it up. Everyone would see it."

"Including the cameras," Ted said. He lowered his weapon. "I hear you're thinking of making a move into politics, General."

The general was quiet for several seconds while he considered it, and Kevin thought he understood some of it now.

"It wouldn't make you look weak," he said. "It would make it look as though you were responsible for giving this to the world. This was sent to Earth, not to one specific country. It's for everyone. It's not something that anyone can own."

General Marquez thought a little more, and then nodded. "Very well." He called out to his men in Spanish, and they lowered their weapons. "We will accompany you to the UN compound, and we will watch this artifact opened up there. You have been very brave, young man."

Kevin felt a flush of pride at that, although one glance back at his mother's face told him just how much trouble he was in for putting himself in harm's way. Ted put an arm around his shoulders, leading him back toward the Jeep.

"Well done," he said, "but don't ever do anything that stupid again. We could have all been killed."

They could have, but they weren't. Better than that, as the trucks started to roll on again in their convoy, they were going toward a place where they might finally find out what it was that the aliens had sent to Earth from their world.

"We're going to get to open the capsule," Kevin said. He couldn't keep the excitement out of his voice.

"We are," Ted agreed, and for once he sounded almost as excited as Kevin. "We're going to see what the aliens sent us."

CHAPTER SIXTEEN

Kevin kept his eyes on the truck that held the capsule all the way back to Bogota. He felt almost like, if he took his eyes off it for a moment, one of the different groups that had spent so much time arguing over it would try to take it.

"It's not going to disappear," Ted said. "You did a good job convincing everyone to work together on this, Kevin."

Kevin wanted to believe it, but the capsule had almost come out of nowhere, hadn't it? Why wouldn't it find a way to disappear the same way? Why wouldn't they be left staring at an empty space, just as they hoped for all the secrets that the aliens had prepared for them?

"It will be okay, Kevin," his mother said, putting a hand on his shoulder. "You've already done the hard part."

Kevin understood that, but even so, he watched the truck. It wasn't just about wanting to make sure nothing happened. It was more the promise of it, and the need to wait. It felt like waiting for Christmas morning and a trip to the doctor's office, all rolled into one. He didn't take his eyes from it until he could see Bogota up ahead.

"The UN facility is just a little further," Ted said, pointing.

The building ahead of them looked about fifty years more modern than most of the buildings around it, built of glass and steel, while the houses that surrounded it seemed kind of quaint and old-fashioned. There was a compound around it, complete with soldiers in blue helmets. They made no move to stop the convoy as it rolled toward the compound, and Kevin guessed that the people in it must have called ahead to let them know what was coming.

That meant that there was no chance of bringing it there quietly. Already, UN staff were standing there, looking at the convoy as it pulled in, while Kevin could see what looked like reporters stuck behind a barrier, barely being kept back by the presence of the soldiers. They pointed cameras, and flashes went off as the convoy ground to a halt. Kevin dared to breathe a sigh of relief. They'd made it here. They had the capsule.

He watched as a group of strong-looking researchers carried it inside, covered with a blanket so that the cameras wouldn't see too much of it.

"I wish they didn't have to hide it away," Kevin said.

Ted looked from the capsule to the cameras. "Something tells me that they won't be able to do it for long. Come on, let's go inside."

Kevin hopped down from the Jeep and then set off with Ted, his mother, and all the others into the UN compound. He wasn't surprised to find more reporters, who had obviously decided to give up the chance for a first picture to be in a better position to shout questions once everyone got inside.

"Is it true?" one shouted. "Have you found an alien spaceship?"

Professor Brewster seemed to think it was obvious that he should answer, stepping forward to do it. "Hello, I'm Professor David Brewster of NASA. We have found *something* out in the rainforest, but for the moment, we're not able to say exactly what it is. My people won't be answering any questions about it at the moment, but there will be a press conference shortly, where we will be publicly examining the artifact that we found."

The press continued to fire questions his way, but Professor Brewster ignored them, walking toward the compound's main building. Kevin and the others hurried to keep up with him.

"We're really going straight into a press conference?" Dr. Levin asked. She didn't sound unhappy about it to Kevin, just surprised.

"Things have progressed quite quickly," Professor Brewster said. "Arguments about who got to work on the rock were becoming quite... vocal."

Kevin had hoped that after everything on the road, the scientists might be able to get along better than that.

"It was decided that the only way to prevent further issues is to deal with the situation here. There will be a press conference to announce it, and, since so many of my colleagues are pushing for it, we will be seeking to cut into the rock to discern the contents."

"You're actually going to open it?" Kevin asked. He hadn't been sure if they would or not.

"Under strictly controlled conditions," Professor Brewster said. "We can't risk potential contamination, either of the rock or the surrounding environment. The room in which we perform the opening will be a sealed space."

He went off to organize it, and Kevin could feel his excitement building.

"They're actually going to open it," he said with a grin. That was so cool.

"And we get to be a part of it," Dr. Levin said.

"Will they need Kevin to be a part of the press conference?" Kevin's mother asked.

"Probably," Dr. Levin said. "He deserves to be, don't you think?"

Kevin's mother nodded. "He does. After all this, he does."

***

The press room was a big conference room, obviously designed to hold large numbers of people. Even so, it felt cramped as Kevin entered it, so packed with reporters and researchers that it was almost impossible to squeeze through them all. A screen had been set up on the far wall, showing a white-walled laboratory, in which the capsule sat on a metal table, flanked by a trio of researchers. They wore white plastic suits that Kevin guessed were to stop them contaminating the capsule. They wore face masks too, and goggles.

At the front of the conference room, there was a long table with a variety of serious-looking men and women sitting behind it. Kevin recognized some of them from their expedition, and General Marquez was at the center of them all. Kevin, Dr. Levin, and Professor Brewster went up to join them.

"Thank you for coming, everyone," Professor Brewster said. "As you probably know by now, we have recently returned from a scientific expedition into Colombia's rainforest. During that expedition, we located the object that you can see."

"What is it?" one reporter called out.

"Where did it come from?" another demanded.

Professor Brewster paused before he answered that. Kevin wondered what it must be like for him, having to say something that sounded impossible, even as he knew that it was true.

"We have reason to believe that this rock is a capsule sent by an alien civilization," Professor Brewster said.

Gasps came from around the room, and all of the reporters started to ask questions at once. Professor Brewster raised his hands for silence.

"You will be aware by now that NASA has been receiving communications from an alien civilization," he said. "These have been decoded by Kevin McKenzie, and based on them, we were able to locate this… object."

He gestured to Kevin, and almost instantly, Kevin found himself blinded by the flashes of dozens of cameras.

"With the cooperation of the Colombian government, and an international team of scientists," Professor Brewster went on, "we recovered the object and brought it here."

He made it sound as if it had all been a lot more peaceful than it was, but Kevin guessed that was the story that they all wanted to tell, of working together and helping one another. It didn't seem like a bad story, if it encouraged people to actually do it next time.

"We are going to perform preliminary tests on the object," Professor Brewster said. "And, subject to the results, of course, we will open the capsule in line with the messages we have received."

Again, a buzz of excitement ran through the room. One certainly ran through Kevin. All this talking was frustrating now. He wanted to get to the point where they actually opened up the capsule and saw what was inside. He tried to imagine what would be in there, but the truth was that it was impossible to imagine. There could be anything from information coded on a hidden supercomputer to vials of living material... anything.

"Kevin," one of the reporters shouted. "What do you think all this will mean? Will you keep getting messages? What impact do you think it will have on humanity?"

"I don't know," Kevin answered. "I guess... I guess I'd like this to be kind of a new start for people. If we know that there are aliens out there, I guess we'll have to think about who we are."

There would be so many changes in the world, and the saddest part of it was that he probably wouldn't be there to see most of them. Even that thought couldn't push aside the excitement. He wanted to see what was inside the rock. He thought just about everyone did, by then.

"If there are no more questions," Professor Brewster said, "we will commence the process of testing."

He signaled to the scientists on the screen, who started to work with devices Kevin didn't know the names of. Kevin found himself holding his breath while they did it.

"X ray seems inconclusive," one of the scientists said. "It might be solid, but it's hard to tell what a normal result should look like for an object like this."

"Spectrometry suggests a composition consistent with a beyond Earth origin," another said. "Similar to several meteorite compositions on our database."

Kevin felt his hopes rise with that, while another ripple of noise went around the room. It seemed that the reporters there wanted to find out what was inside the capsule just as much as he did. Or almost as much, at least. Kevin couldn't imagine anyone wanting to know as much as he did then.

"Given our preliminary data," Professor Brewster asked the scientists on the screen, "is there any reason why we should not attempt to open the object?"

To Kevin, he sounded like he was trying to sound as calm and authoritative as possible. Kevin mostly just wished that they'd hurry up. He wasn't sure how much longer he could sit there, waiting for them to do the one thing that they all knew they wanted to do.

"There are no obvious dangers," the scientist on the other end of the video link said. "The structure of the rock appears sufficient to survive the process, and the appropriate safety precautions are in place."

It sounded like a very long-winded way of saying that they could do it, to Kevin, but the main thing was that they *were* saying it.

"Very well," Professor Brewster said. "Begin cutting into the object."

He nodded to the scientists on the screen, and they went over to the rock, clamping it in place so that they could work on it. One came back with an electric saw that looked too big for one person to hold. It looked like the kind of thing that could cut through concrete or metal with ease.

Kevin half-expected it to bounce off the surface of the rock in spite of that. He thought that an alien capsule tough enough to make it all the way from the Trappist 1 system should be tough enough to stand up to a saw.

The saw bit into it, though, sparks and dust flying as it chewed through the rock.

"We're getting some resistance," one of the researchers said. "We might have to switch to a heavier blade."

They kept going, first making an incision around the rock as if expecting it to fall open like an Easter egg the moment they did so, then plowing into it with the saw when that didn't happen. They kept going until dust almost filled the screen, only clearing slowly, showing two halves of the capsule split neatly.

Kevin stared at that image, and he guessed that everyone else there and around the world was staring in that moment, trying to make sense of it. He looked at it until his eyes hurt, trying to pick out the details that would tell him what the aliens had sent to them. What was inside the capsule? What had been so important that they'd sent it light years away, to a completely different world?

He stared at it in hope first, then in disbelief.

What he was seeing simply didn't make sense.

CHAPTER SEVENTEEN

Around the room, Kevin could hear the murmuring of the scientists and the reporters as they started to realize the same thing Kevin did.

The inside of the "capsule" was just a solid, rocky surface. There was no hollow, no sign of any advanced technology. The rock that the scientists had just cut through was…

…well, it was a rock.

Instantly, there was uproar, as a hundred reporters shouted questions simultaneously. On the screen, the scientists were looking just as shocked, standing there as if they didn't know what to do next.

"How would you like us to proceed, Professor Brewster?" one asked. "Professor Brewster?"

He didn't answer. From what Kevin could see, he was too busy standing there red-faced, not knowing how to respond.

"Professor Brewster, what's going on?" a journalist called out above the others.

"Is this some kind of joke?" another managed to shout.

"Why is this rock empty?" a third yelled.

Kevin could see Professor Brewster looking around as if there were someone who might have all the answers for him. He looked so embarrassed in that moment that Kevin actually felt sorry for him.

"I… I don't…" Professor Brewster said. He shook his head. "I'm sorry, but there has been some kind of mistake…"

***

Kevin had never been as disappointed as he felt on the flight back to San Francisco with the others. They were going to head back to the institute, because they had equipment to take back, and because Professor Brewster had said something about wanting to do a proper debrief there. Right then, though, a part of Kevin just wanted to run home and hide.

He sat there, hoping for the sensation that would come before a signal, hoping that there would be some kind of answer, an explanation, but there was nothing. There hadn't been for so long now it was hard to remember that the signals had been real, that they hadn't just been a figment of his imagination. He huddled in on himself, not sure what to think, or what to do right then.

Perhaps it was the headphones, but no one bothered him there. His mother sat beside him on the plane. Everyone else seemed to keep their distance, even people like Phil, Ted, and Dr. Levin, as if someone had warned them against getting too close, telling them that it would hurt them now by association with Kevin's failure.

It *was* his. He'd been the one to decode all the signals. He'd been the one to lead them to South America, and then to the spot where the meteorite lay in the small lake. Something had gone wrong somewhere, and Kevin couldn't help feeling that he'd been the one to get it wrong.

"Don't blame yourself," his mother insisted, obviously guessing what Kevin was thinking about. "You couldn't know it would turn out like this. Maybe we should all have been more careful about going along with it."

That sounded as though his mother was blaming herself for ever taking Kevin to SETI in the first place. Maybe she was thinking that she should have been firmer about it.

"I don't know what went wrong, Mom," Kevin said. "I mean, I *heard* the signals. And we found the capsule right where they said it would be."

"We found *something*," his mother corrected him gently. "Maybe we were all so eager to find it that we assumed we knew what it would be. We all got ourselves convinced."

Except that it had been Kevin who had convinced them, because he'd been the one hearing the signals. They *were* real. They'd come through the institute's listening equipment. Everyone had heard them. If so, why hadn't the capsule been where it should be?

"What will happen to the capsule now?" Kevin asked.

"I don't know," his mother said. "I think I saw them loading it onto the plane. I guess no one cares who owns it now that it's just a rock. That doesn't matter right now, though. The important thing is that we get you back safely."

Something about the way she said that told Kevin that his mother was worried about being able to do it. She sounded as though she was expecting trouble, and Kevin couldn't understand why.

He understood once they landed, though, stepping down from the plane and then out into the arrival lounge. Almost as soon as they did, a wall of voices hit him, camera flashes going off everywhere.

"Why did you do it, Kevin?" one reporter called out.

"Tell us all that it's not a hoax!" a man near the back shouted.

"We believed in you!"

There were reporters there, but there were other people too, some with placards, some just shouting. None of them looked happy to see Kevin there. They mobbed around the scientists, pressing in as they started to unload their gear. The meteorite was in amongst it somewhere. Now that there was no sign of aliens, no one cared if they took it back to the NASA facility.

"Is it right that the public pays for all this when you are going off to Colombia to chase rocks?" one reporter called out. "Don't you think that this is a waste of money that could be spent on schools or the military?"

People came forward, still shouting questions, and for a moment or two, Kevin found them pressing in on all sides. He lost sight of his mother in the crush, and then it was like he was drowning in the camera flashes, the questions coming so fast as to be almost deafening.

"Why did you lie, Kevin?"

"Was this just to get attention?"

"Was it all about your illness?"

Kevin kept his head down, not knowing what to say. He looked for a way through the mob, but everywhere he looked there were people looking at him with accusing expressions. Some grabbed for him; not the reporters, but they were happy enough to take pictures as the people with the signs did it.

"Fraud! Liar!"

Kevin huddled in further, and he felt as though at any minute he might fall to the ground under the weight of them all, pushed down by the sheer numbers of people around him. Another hand fastened onto him, but this one kept hold, pulling him through the crush. Kevin saw Ted there, pushing back anyone who got too close, his hand up to get in the way of the camera flashes.

"Keep moving!" he called out above the noise. "There's a car waiting outside!"

Kevin did his best, not stopping as Ted carved a path through the reporters like someone pushing their way through deep snow. Kevin hurried to fit into that space before it closed up again, following as they fought their way forward, toward the airport's main entrance.

"Out here!" Ted said, pointing to where a minivan stood waiting, Kevin's mother and half a dozen scientists already inside. There was a brief moment of space there, and Kevin ran for the vehicle, jumping in beside his mother. She clung to him as if afraid that if she let go he would disappear. For once, Kevin didn't complain.

Ted drove, fitting into a convoy of vehicles that felt as tense, in some ways, as the one through the rainforest had. Kevin saw cars drive up close, their windows rolling down to reveal more cameras, but Ted kept driving.

It seemed to take forever before they reached the NASA facility. The crowds that had surrounded it before were still there, but now they weren't curious, they were angry. Kevin could hear them shouting as they drove in, and when Ted stopped in front of the doors to the institute, Kevin ran inside without hesitation. He didn't even try to talk to them, to explain. He wasn't sure that he *had* an explanation. Instead, Kevin just ran back to his room in the facility. He ignored his mother when she followed, sitting there hoping that somehow, some of it would make sense.

When it didn't, he went to one of the recreation rooms and used a computer there to call the one person who might understand what was happening to him.

Luna looked worried when Kevin called, and Kevin could guess why.

"You saw the broadcast," he said.

"I think *everyone* saw the broadcast," Luna replied. "I don't get it. I thought that there was supposed to be some special... I don't know, *alien stuff.*"

"I thought so too," Kevin said. "Now... I'm *sure* I got the signals right."

"Don't start that," Luna said, in her firm voice. "Don't start doubting all of this. I was there when you saw the numbers, remember? I know that this is real."

It felt good to be believed, particularly by Luna. There was something reassuringly *solid* about Luna's belief. It was the kind that people could have built on, unwavering and strong. Kevin needed that right then.

"You might not want to go back to your house right now," Luna said. "You know how there have been reporters around it since this started?"

Kevin nodded.

"Well, now there are like twice as many, plus a bunch of other people who don't look happy. It's like a mob or something."

"It's because I gave them a dream," Kevin said. "And they think that I lied to them."

"Well, they shouldn't blame you," Luna said. "I mean, I was watching that broadcast. That Professor Brewster *himself* said the rock was from outer space."

That wasn't enough, though, was it?

"I don't think that will make things better," Kevin said. "They'll say it was just some random meteorite. There are plenty of those."

In fact, he suspected that it would make things worse, because if there was one person who didn't like being made to look stupid, it was...

"Kevin," his mother called from the doorway. She was standing there with Phil. "You need to come with us. Professor Brewster wants to speak with you and me."

Kevin swallowed, because that sounded far too much like when the principal wanted to talk to someone at school.

"Looks like I have to go," Kevin said to Luna.

"Okay," Luna replied. "Just remember, this isn't your fault."

Kevin tried to remember that as he made his way with his mother and Phil through the facility. Ordinarily the researcher might have joked around, but now he had a serious look, and barely said anything, just opening the doors ahead of them as he had to. When they got to Professor Brewster's office, Phil didn't say anything, just turned and left.

"What was that about?" Kevin asked his mother.

"I think a lot of people are hurt by how angry people are at them," she said. "They all believed that they would find aliens and... they didn't, Kevin." She took his hand. "You've got to be prepared. I... I don't think this will be good."

They went into Professor Brewster's office. He was waiting for them, sitting behind his desk, looking formal, even imposing. He didn't say hello as they came in, just gestured for Kevin and his mother to sit down in two chairs in front of his desk.

"Kevin," he said, "Ms. McKenzie, we need to talk." He paused, looking at Kevin as if trying to see into him. "Kevin, I need to ask you, did you make all of this up?"

"How dare you ask my son that?" his mother demanded, half rising out of her chair. "Kevin is not a liar."

"Please sit down, Ms. McKenzie," Professor Brewster said. "Kevin, did you make this up?"

Kevin couldn't believe that he was asking that.

"No," Kevin said, shaking his head.

"Are you sure?"

"This is uncalled for," Kevin's mother said. "You have no right to ask this."

Professor Brewster steepled his fingers. "Given the amount of money that the government has put into this project, not only do I have the right to ask it, I have the *obligation*. Kevin?"

"You heard the signals," Kevin said. "I didn't make it up!"

"I heard signals, yes," Professor Brewster said. "But you were the only one who could 'translate' them, and space is full of electromagnetic oddities."

"I didn't make it up," Kevin said. "I gave you the numbers for the coordinates. I gave you information about the planets that no one else knew."

"Which you could have memorized," Professor Brewster said. He looked at Kevin's mother. "Maybe you were coached."

"Are you accusing me of something?" Kevin's mother shot back.

"I'm just noting the possibility," Professor Brewster said. He sighed. "As are many other people. The truth is that you came to us and we threw resources at you that we should not have. We provided you with healthcare, testing… and now I have important people calling me to ask if that was all a trick."

"It wasn't," Kevin insisted. Why were people not believing him now?

"Then why was there nothing but rock when we cut into that 'capsule' of yours?" Professor Brewster asked.

"I… don't know," Kevin admitted. There should have been more. He didn't understand it. "You said that it was from space."

He saw Professor Brewster wince at that. "Don't remind me. I put my reputation on the line in backing you, Kevin. I stood up in front of people and told them that you were real. But many rocks are from space. At any one time, the Earth is peppered by fragments from space. We have meteorite hunters who sell them over the Internet. The fact is that this one didn't have any evidence of the aliens you promised."

Kevin tried to remember what Luna had said. "That isn't my fault."

Professor Brewster put his hands flat on the table, shaking his head. "The truth is, that doesn't matter at this point," he said. "The fact is that your presence here has become toxic for this facility. Powerful people were expecting results from us, and we weren't able to deliver them. Already, I've had calls suggesting that our funding will be cut if we don't sever all ties with you at once."

Kevin tried to make sense of that. "You... you're sending me away?"

Professor Brewster was stony-faced. "I don't know if you faked all this or not, but I'll say this: already, the FBI is looking into whether you and your mother have committed crimes through your actions here. The best thing that you can do right now is to leave, both of you. You will take nothing with you, and you will receive a bill in due course for any medical services we provided."

"Come on, Kevin," his mother said. "We're leaving."

She managed to make it sound like something they were choosing to do, rather than something they'd just been all but ordered to do. She marched angrily along the corridors that led from the building, and if Kevin hadn't been able to see the tears at the corners of her eyes, he might have believed that she really was just furious and not hurt.

They walked past Dr. Levin, who half turned away from them. Kevin stopped in front of her, hoping she might be able to work all of this out.

"Dr. Levin..." he began.

The SETI director didn't give him any time to finish. "I'm sorry, Kevin. I heard what happened."

"You could talk to Professor Brewster," he said.

Dr. Levin shook her head. "I don't think David would listen to me right now. I lost a lot of my credibility around here, bringing you to them."

"But I'm not making this up," Kevin insisted.

Dr. Levin sighed. "I know you believe that, Kevin," she said. "It's just... maybe I should have checked things more carefully. Maybe you found out about things another way, and didn't even realize."

"I didn't," Kevin insisted.

His mother took his arm. "Come on, Kevin. We're done here. We're going to go home."

She led him away from Dr. Levin, and when Kevin looked back at the scientist, Dr. Levin wouldn't look at him. The two of them kept going to the exit and out through it, into the noise of the questions being shouted from every angle.

To his surprise, Ted was waiting there, standing by Kevin's mother's car. He must have brought it around for them.

"Are you here to question my son's honesty too?" Kevin's mother asked, moving between him and Ted.

To Kevin's surprise, or maybe not, Ted shook his head. "Nothing like that. I just wanted to talk to him."

Kevin's mother looked as though she wasn't sure, but Kevin put a hand on her arm.

"It's okay, Mom," he said. "I trust Ted."

He'd trusted lots of the scientists too, though. He looked up at Ted.

"I didn't make this up," he said.

"I never said you did," Ted replied. "People change what they think to fit in. They get disappointed because things don't work out, and they look for someone to blame. They start thinking that proof they've seen with their own eyes must be a trick."

He held out his hand and Kevin took it. "Thanks, Ted."

"You stay safe," Ted said. "And... try not to let the things they're going to say get to you too much, okay?"

"Okay," Kevin promised.

He couldn't see how he could avoid it, though. He'd promised the world aliens and he'd failed.

He'd *failed.*

Was he a fraud, after all? Had he unconsciously imagined the entire thing?

CHAPTER EIGHTEEN

There were reporters surrounding Kevin's house when they got back. Reporters, and protestors, and even a few police, obviously there to keep the rest of them back. Kevin kept his head down in the passenger's seat of his mother's car, hoping that no one would see him, but there was no real hope of that. The moment they saw the car pulling up, the mass of people surrounded it, and the car practically shone with the glare of the camera flashes.

"When I open your door, don't stop," his mother said. She got out, and Kevin braced himself.

She pulled open the door on his side, wrapping a protective arm around Kevin even though he was taller than she was.

"Get back," she yelled at them. "Get off my property."

The reporters pulled back a little, but the press of people barely slackened. Kevin held tight to his mother as they fought their way through. The cops there yelled for people to get back, but they didn't make any move to help the two of them physically. Kevin got the feeling that they were probably just as upset as everybody else about what had happened. How many of them had believed that they were about to talk to aliens directly? How many of them now hated him because the capsule hadn't been what they expected?

He and his mother pushed their way forward anyway, shoving past people who grabbed at them, demanding answers to questions Kevin didn't *have* an answer for.

"Why weren't there aliens?"

"Why did you do all this?"

"Do you know how many people you've hurt?"

Kevin saw his mother turn to them angrily, and he tried to pull her back, but it was too late to do anything about it.

"Leave my boy alone!" she shouted. "He hasn't done anything wrong here. He's ill!"

They pushed their way into the house, shutting the door behind them. Kevin saw his mother bolting it the way she might have if she thought that people were going to try to break in. She went through the house, drawing the curtains, blocking out the flashes of the photographers along with the light.

Kevin went over to the TV, turning it on. The news was running, with pictures of their house from the outside, and a short clip of his mother that made her look like a madwoman as she pushed reporters back.

"Leave my boy alone. He hasn't done anything wrong here. He's ill!"

The words *An admission of the hoax?* played across the bottom of the screen, in a question that managed to accuse without accusing. They made it sound as if Kevin's mother were trying to excuse him doing something wrong, rather than standing up for him as she had been.

She had been, hadn't she?

"You should turn that off," his mother said. She stepped past Kevin, doing exactly that, sending the screen into darkness. "It won't do any good watching them saying all this about you."

"Mom," Kevin said, "what they're saying... They're making it sound like you don't really believe me. Like you think I'm making things up because I'm ill."

His mother didn't answer for a moment or two.

"You do think that," Kevin said. He couldn't believe it. He'd thought that his mother, of all people, would believe him at this point.

"I don't know what to think, Kevin," his mother said. She sounded so tired then. "I know that you believe all this."

"We found the signal," Kevin insisted. "You defended me to Professor Brewster."

"You're my son," his mother said. "I won't let them say bad things about you, no matter what happens. Whether it's true or not... I don't know. I was convinced, but everything with the rock..."

Kevin felt sick inside. He felt as though things were back to where they had been when his mother had first taken him to SETI, doing it only because she thought it was something Kevin needed to do. He didn't want her to do things because she was his mother and she felt she had to. He wanted her to believe him.

"They'll go away eventually," his mother said. "They'll forget about all of this. We can get on with our lives without them, without aliens, without any of it."

She sounded as though she was trying to reassure Kevin, but Kevin wasn't sure that it was all that reassuring.

He might have said just that, but his mother's phone rang then.

"Hello," she said. "Who is... No, I don't have anything to say to you or any other reporter."

She'd barely hung up before there was another call, and another. Each time, she hung up after only a few seconds of

119

conversation. When the phone rang again, Kevin thought that his mother might throw her phone across the room. She paused as she held it up though, looking at the screen with a worried expression.

"What is it, Mom?" Kevin asked.

"It's work," his mother said, and something about the way she said that told Kevin just how scared she was. She took the call, gesturing for Kevin to be quiet. "Hello, Mr. Banks. Yes, it is pretty bad. Yes, I know I've been off, but my son… yes, I know. No, I understand that, but… You can't do that. I know it's bad publicity, but you can't…" She fell silent, listening for several seconds. "No, I understand."

She finished the call, and this time she *did* throw her phone, sitting down on the edge of the sofa, her head in her hands.

"Mom?" Kevin said, reaching out for her. "What happened?"

"That was my work," she said, without looking up. "They… they fired me. They said that they don't want the negative publicity that might come from employing someone linked to all this."

"Can they do that?" Kevin asked. It didn't sound like the kind of thing people should be allowed to do, especially when they'd done nothing wrong.

"They say they can," his mother said, "and if I fight it, well, I'm pretty sure that they'd make it so expensive I couldn't do anything, and maybe a judge would agree that I'm causing their business problems by being there anyway."

It didn't sound fair to Kevin. It didn't sound right. Worse, it didn't sound as though there was anything they could do about it.

"I'm sorry, Mom," he said. "If I'd just kept all this to myself…"

"It isn't your fault," his mother said.

Kevin knew that wasn't true, though. Thanks to the TV, he knew his mother didn't even think that. He'd gone to NASA talking about aliens, and now his mom was getting fired, while no one even believed him about what he'd heard.

"It will be okay," his mother said. She didn't sound as though she believed it. "We'll find a way to make all of this right."

She sat there on the sofa, not putting the TV on, neither of them daring to open the curtains. Eventually, Kevin went up to his room, sitting there in the dark so his mother wouldn't worry about him quite as much.

After a while, he took out the headphones that Ted had given him before he left the institute, putting them on more to shut out the sounds of the reporters outside than because he truly thought something would happen. Maybe he did hope for it. If he could get

120

another message that would help to make sense of all this, maybe he could go out to the reporters there and explain it all. Maybe he could make people understand again that it *was* real, and that he *hadn't* been lying.

There was only silence, though. No signal, no words in his head, no sign of anything that would help. Taking off the headphones, Kevin threw them aside and settled down to sleep. Maybe in the morning, things would look better.

***

Kevin went over to his bedroom window, looking out the way he might have if he'd been looking for snow anywhere other than California. He was looking for journalists, hoping that by now, several days later, they would have gotten bored with waiting around the house and gone home.

They hadn't. There were still cameras out there in front of the house, still reporters with microphones waiting for whatever the next step would be in their story. Kevin wished that they would go away, and thought for the hundredth time about going down there to tell them to do just that, but he didn't. It wasn't the same thing as translating the messages while people watched in a press conference, and anyway, Kevin suspected that was just what they were waiting for.

Instead, he went to get dressed, and staggered slightly as a wave of dizziness hit him. Pain followed, flaring through his skull, and Kevin felt wetness against his lips. When he put his hand to his nose, it came away red with blood. He even *felt* sicker today, the effort of going to the bathroom and cleaning up almost exhausting him.

He still did it though. He didn't want to worry his mother. He made sure that he looked okay when he went downstairs, and tried to hide the faint tremor in his hands that wouldn't go away now.

He hadn't realized until then just how much care he'd been getting in the research institute. He'd complained about all the tests and the scans and the rest, but maybe somewhere in all of that there had been something that had been slowing down his illness. Or maybe he'd just been so busy he hadn't noticed its progression.

"I can't worry Mom," he told himself.

When he went downstairs, he could hear voices.

"I'm sorry, Ms. McKenzie, but this is not a joke. Proceedings are being brought against you for using your son to defraud people, and we need to take them seriously."

Kevin hurried down there, and saw a couple of people in suits talking to his mother. She looked as though she hadn't slept at all, and when she looked over at Kevin, he could see the purple shadows around her eyes.

"Ah, here's your son now," one of the men said. "Maybe we could take a statement from him now, and that might help."

"No," his mother said, "not now, not like this. I just want people to leave my son alone."

"I don't mind, Mom," Kevin said.

"Well, I do," his mother said. "Go into the kitchen, Kevin. I need to talk to these people."

If she'd shouted, Kevin might have argued. Instead, she just sounded incredibly sad, and Kevin did as she asked, going through to the kitchen and sitting there at the kitchen table. All the time, he tried to listen to what was happening through the walls.

"I'll have to sell the house," his mother said. "What this will cost... I can't think of another way."

"I understand that this is difficult, Ms. McKenzie, but it is important that we deal with it. The alternative could involve imprisonment, for you, or for your son."

Kevin's fingers gripped the edge of the kitchen table hard enough that it hurt. They couldn't do it, could they? They couldn't throw his mother in jail, when he'd been telling the truth. He sat there, part of him wanting to burst in there, part of him knowing that it was all far too important to do that.

He was still sitting there when he saw the figure sneaking into their backyard, a beanie hat covering their head, a thick coat pulled up to obscure their features. They leapt over with the grace of someone who had done that kind of thing plenty of times before, landing neatly in the yard.

If it had been a reporter or some stranger clambering over the fence, he didn't know what he would have done. Called for help, probably. Interrupted his mother in spite of the seriousness of what was happening. Instead, he unlocked the back door, letting Luna into the house as she hurried over.

"Hey," she said, hugging him so suddenly that it almost took Kevin by surprise.

"Hey," Kevin replied. "I'm guessing you couldn't get here the front way?"

"Too many reporters," Luna agreed, stepping back. She pulled away the beanie cap. "Like my disguise?"

"It's great," Kevin said, but he couldn't bring himself to smile.

"What's wrong?" Luna asked. She shook her head. "Stupid question."

Kevin went to sit back down, Luna joining him. How many times had they done their homework like that? This felt different, though, more serious.

"There are lawyers in the other room," he said. "They're saying that my mom might go to jail, and that we might have to sell the house."

"What for?" Luna demanded, in the kind of indignant tone that said she was ready to fight them off, lawyers or not. "You didn't do anything wrong."

"They think I did," Kevin said. "They think… I guess they think that I made all of this up to get attention, or to con them into giving me medical treatment, or something."

"Then they're idiots," Luna declared, with the kind of iron-hard certainty that no one else around him seemed to have. "You gave them messages from another world. You told them all about a planet they would barely know anything about otherwise. You helped them *find* the meteorite thing, even if it was empty. It isn't your fault that aliens are weird and send rocks to people as presents."

That was a way of looking at it Kevin suspected that nobody other than Luna could manage. Even so, it felt good.

"So, you believe me?" he asked.

She nodded. "I believe you. I believe *in* you too. You'll find a way to deal with this."

"And you climbed over my fence just to tell me that?" Kevin asked.

Luna put a hand on his shoulder. "What are friends for? I like sneaking in. It's fun. Besides, I need to take you somewhere."

Kevin looked back at her in surprise.

"Where?" he asked.

She smiled wide.

"It's a surprise."

CHAPTER NINETEEN

Kevin checked how he looked in the mirror before heading out. It wasn't vanity; he wanted to make sure that there was no possible way anyone could recognize him. He had his hoodie pulled up over his head, dark glasses on to break up some of the lines of his face. It wasn't great, but if he hunched in enough then he could almost convince himself that people wouldn't be able to tell that it was him.

"It will have to do," he said to himself.

His mother had left the house a few minutes before, out talking to more lawyers, or maybe trying to find another job, not that anyone wanted to hire the mother of the boy who'd lied. The doors were locked against the continued presence of the reporters out front, and would probably stay that way even after she got back.

"She'll be mad if she finds out I did this," Kevin said, but that was part of why he was wearing the disguise. He'd been sitting in the house too long, with no school because of his illness, no chance of going out because of both the reporters and his mother's fear of what might happen. He was going crazy there, and he suspected that was only making things harder for his mother. He needed to get outside at least for a while.

His phone was full of messages from people he didn't know. Some were questions, more were insults. One or two held threats, or promises that they would pay Kevin if only he would tell them his story.

Kevin wasn't sure that he wanted to be careful then. He felt as though he might explode if he stayed hiding out for much longer. He looked out the back, trying to judge if he could get out of there the same way Luna had gotten in. A few weeks ago, he wouldn't have had to worry about it.

Now, he thought about the tremors that came and went in his body, the moments of losing time and the dizzy spells. He fetched a stepladder from where his mother kept it in the garage, setting it up against the fence and using that to climb over, to a small path that ran between yards.

Kevin kept his head down as he went along, making sure that no one saw his face. Even though the part of town where he lived wasn't a bad one, it was just a few blocks to a more industrial area,

124

where factories stuck up like fenced-in boxes, and occasional rusted out machinery pointed to the businesses that hadn't done so well.

"Come on," Luna said, after they hopped the fence, setting off at a walk that took them through some of the abandoned buildings, past graffiti that looked as though it had been painted with someone's eyes shut.

They came out closer to the center of town. Kevin kept his hood up, sure that even here, away from his house, people would spot him.

"We could go to the mall," Luna suggested.

Kevin shook his head. "Too many people."

"The square then," Luna suggested.

Kevin nodded. There might be almost as many people there in the middle of town, but they would be moving on more, less likely to notice a kid keeping his head down. In the mall, security would probably think he was there to steal something, but out in the open, he and Luna could walk where they wanted without it being a problem.

They headed into the heart of town, for a small square where they and their friends had hung out since they were kids. There was a smaller block of park there, with trees at each corner, and a statue in the middle that had probably once been a monument to someone very important, but had now been worn by the wind and rain until it could have been anyone. By the time they got there, Kevin was so exhausted that he started looking around for a bench to sit down on.

"Kevin," Luna said, "what's wrong?"

"I'm just tired," Kevin said.

Luna frowned, obviously not believing it. "Well, we could always go to Frankie's."

The diner had been one of their favorite places for a long time. Maybe if he hadn't been so exhausted, Kevin might have been worried by that, but as it was, he could do with somewhere to recover a little from the effort of the walk. He nodded.

"I thought you managed to go trekking through the jungle," Luna said.

"I think things are getting worse," Kevin said, as they made their way toward the diner. "It's like I have to concentrate to make my body do things."

Even that wasn't putting it right, but he wasn't sure there were words for it. That was one of the hardest parts about having such a rare illness: it meant there weren't really the words to describe everything that was happening.

"You should go to the hospital," Luna said, and she sounded as if she wanted to call for an ambulance right away.

Kevin shook his head. "There's no point. We know what's happening to me. It's not as though they can do much to help."

"That can't be true," Luna said. For a moment, Kevin heard her voice catch and he thought that maybe she might cry. "I know… I know they can't cure you, but they can help with the symptoms and things, right? They can slow things down? They were doing it in the NASA place."

"Because they had some of the cleverest scientists in the world," Kevin pointed out. "I don't think they're going to want to help now. And… if I go to the hospital now, I think it would cost too much. I don't think Mom could really afford my treatment even before all this. Now, with the lawyers and stuff…"

Kevin didn't know how much a court case cost. A lot, he guessed. His treatment cost a lot too. Was that twice a lot, then? A lot squared? When he had no idea of the amounts involved, his imagination couldn't even begin to supply the amounts.

"Okay," Luna said, "but we should at least get inside. Come on, Frankie's isn't far."

They went into the diner, which wasn't busy at that time of day. There were a few kids Kevin half recognized, a couple of older guys in one corner, and the owner, a fifty-something man who seemed to spend most of his time wiping down the counter with a cloth. It was a deliberately old-fashioned kind of place, and it should have meant that Kevin's friends didn't like it, but it also had great ice cream.

"I'll go get ice cream," Luna said, pointing to a corner booth. "You sit down."

She made that into an order, and Kevin did it. He needed to sit down anyway, and if it meant that Luna was buying the ice cream, that was even better. There was a TV on in the corner of the diner, and for a moment or two, Kevin thought that was okay. Then the news came on, and the pictures of the scenes around his house continued.

Kevin did his best to ignore it, but it wasn't easy. That the channel was still there at all was kind of surprising; maybe someone still believed, or maybe they just hadn't gotten around to looking at something else yet. Either way, he sat there, hunched in on himself. It was hard to imagine that just a few weeks ago, he and Luna had come here regularly; that everything had been normal. Now, he was sitting here, and as far as Kevin could tell he was pretty much just waiting to die.

That was a thought he didn't want, but it crept in when he wasn't looking, sitting down in his mind and refusing to budge, no matter how he pushed at it. He was going to die. He'd been able to ignore that while there had still been all the stuff with the aliens, the messages, and the trip to the rainforest. Now, there was nothing to do but sit there and think about it.

"Well," Luna said, coming back with two glasses filled to the brim with ice cream, "you look miserable. Better cheer up, or you're not getting ice cream."

Only Luna would make fun of him when he was like this. Only Luna would know that it was exactly what Kevin needed.

"You're just looking for an excuse to have both," Kevin said.

Luna smiled. "Maybe. You're still stuck thinking about what you could have done differently?"

Kevin nodded. "I don't know why. I guess... I just keep hoping it will make sense."

"Hope is good," Luna said. "I think it's good you're still listening. You shouldn't give up, even if people don't believe you."

Kevin nodded. He needed this. He needed something to hold onto, otherwise—

"Hey, wait, you're Kevin McKenzie, aren't you? The boy who made up all that alien stuff? You used to go to our school."

Kevin looked over to find that some of the kids were looking his way. He was about to tell them that he didn't want trouble, but Luna was already on her feet, moving toward them.

"Kevin didn't make anything up!"

"Of course he made it up," one boy said. "Who would be stupid enough to believe in aliens?"

"You and everyone else, apparently," Luna snapped.

"Are you calling me stupid?"

Kevin got up, joining her. "We don't want any trouble."

"So why did you do it then?" a girl at the back demanded. "My parents were so worried about aliens coming that they were talking about selling our house and moving out into the countryside."

More people were staring at them now, and people had their phones out. Kevin knew he couldn't be seen here like this. His mom would go crazy. Besides, he'd seen what large groups of people could be like.

"We'll just go," Kevin said, holding up his hands. "We don't want to cause a problem."

"You're not going anywhere," the boy who'd spoken first said. "Not until you admit what you did."

He stood there with his arms folded, looking like he meant it. That was a problem, because the longer they stayed there, the more people would be watching. Luna seemed to be thinking the same thing, and, being Luna, she took a more direct approach to the problem:

She walked up to the boy in the doorway and pushed him, hard.

"Run, Kevin!"

She was already running, and it took Kevin a moment to realize he should be doing the same, but *only* a moment. As tired as he had been, he was recovered enough now to run past the boy, following Luna as she ran out into the middle of the town. He ran as fast as he could, ignoring the way his breath came in short bursts, trying to keep up as they retraced their steps, heading back through the factories and past the rusting metal. Kevin ran until he felt that his heart might explode in his chest, his lungs burning.

When it was obvious that no one was following, he and Luna came to a halt, and to his surprise, Kevin found himself laughing.

Luna laughed too. "That was *fun*."

"My mom is going to kill me," Kevin pointed out, but right then, even that didn't sound so bad. The truth was that he felt better than he had for days now. It felt like so long since he'd done something as simple as getting into trouble with Luna, running away before it could turn into anything worse.

"Your mom will be fine with it," Luna said.

"I'm not so sure about that," Kevin replied, because she would be angry that he'd gone out like that, angry that he'd risked everything by going where people might see him. "When I get home, I'm going to have to…"

He trailed off as a feeling started to rise through him. A feeling he knew far too well, because it had been there before the facility, before NASA, before all of it.

"What is it?" Luna said. "What are you going to have to do?"

Kevin shook his head. "Luna, I think…"

"What?" she said.

"I think there's another message coming through."

CHAPTER TWENTY

Kevin stood among the factories, listening to the transmission as it started to come. He struggled to latch onto the message. That was hard at first; harder than it had been, and harder than Kevin suspected it should be.

He started to worry. What if whatever it was in his brain that connected with the transmissions had changed, shifting with the slow progress of his illness? What if there had only been a brief window when his brain was receptive to it all, and now it was starting to pass beyond it? He tried to concentrate, focusing on the sounds and willing them to make sense.

An image burned in his brain, numbers shining there in neat rows of coordinates. Kevin wouldn't have recognized them as that, but he'd seen strings of them before, when he'd known to shift the telescope the first time to pick up the stream of the message.

"Kevin?" Luna said. "Are you all right?"

Kevin didn't know how to answer that. The strange part was that he felt better than he'd felt in days, maybe some interaction between his illness and the message making the symptoms feel better for the moment.

"I don't know," he said. "I think… I think the aliens want us to look for signals in a new place."

It was what they'd wanted the last time he'd had a signal through straight to his brain like this, the power of it almost impossible to hold. It had been the beginning of all of this.

"So who do we tell?" Luna asked.

Kevin must have stared at her too long in the wake of that, because she spread her hands.

"What? We have to tell *someone*," she said.

Kevin knew she was probably right. If there was a fresh message, people would want to know. The problem was that he wasn't sure how they would react. He'd seen all the reporters who were still outside of his house. He'd seen the pain that it had caused his mother. Wouldn't it be better to just keep quiet and protect her?

"I'm not sure if anyone will believe me," he said. "They think that I'm a fake. If I tell people, then they'll assume that I'm just trying to get attention."

People wouldn't listen to him now, whatever he said. If he came forward with another string of numbers, wouldn't they assume that he was just trying to start it all again?

"We could tell your mom," Luna said. "She'd believe you, and she'd know what to do."

Kevin shook his head. "I'm not sure she would now, not after all the trouble this has caused. Even if she did, I don't know if anyone would listen to her, either."

"Who then?" Luna asked. "We have to tell *someone*. A reporter, maybe?"

That would at least get the news out into the open, but again, it didn't feel like the right idea. If he went to the reporters, trying to explain, wouldn't they just make fun of it? He needed to be able to prove it. There was only one place he could do that, only one place where they might be able to realign a telescope to pick up whatever new signal awaited.

"We need to contact someone at the NASA facility," Kevin said.

Even as he said it, he could guess how difficult that might be. He took out his phone, trying to think of the best way to do it. It wasn't as though he had direct numbers for any of the people who might be able to help.

He decided to start with Dr. Levin, because at least the SETI director had seemed more sympathetic than Professor Brewster. He found a number for SETI online and called it, listening to it ring and finally getting through to reception.

"Hello," the receptionist said. "SETI Institute. How can I help you?"

"I need to speak to Dr. Levin about an urgent matter," Kevin said, trying to sound as grown up as he could. Maybe if he could make it sound as though he was a colleague or something, they might let him speak to her.

"Who is this?" the receptionist asked.

"Well… um…" Kevin looked over at Luna, who shrugged. "This is Kevin McKenzie. But I have to speak to her right away. There's been another message, and there's a second set of coordinates, and…"

He heard the click as the receptionist hung up.

"They wouldn't even let me explain," Kevin said. That hurt, that after so much they would hang up without even letting him say anything.

"We need to keep trying," Luna insisted. "Here, let me. We'll try NASA. They've got the telescopes, after all."

130

She rang, and pressed some buttons. It seemed that she did a better job of sounding older too, because when she spoke, it sounded to Kevin more like her mother than it did his friend.

"Hello, I was wondering if you could put me through to Professor Brewster? It's quite urgent, yes. It's Professor Sophie Langford of the University of Wisconsin. Yes, I'll hold."

Kevin hadn't known that Luna was quite that good at making things up on the spot. She thrust her phone at him, and Kevin took it, just in time for Professor Brewster's voice to come onto the other end of the line.

"Hello?" Professor Brewster said. "Professor... Langford, was it?"

Kevin took a breath. "Professor Brewster, it's me, Kevin. Don't hang up, it's urgent."

"What are you doing calling this number?" Professor Brewster demanded. "And getting through to me under false pretenses? Don't you think you're in enough trouble already, young man?"

"Listen to me," Kevin said. "I wouldn't be calling if it weren't important. There are things you need to know."

"I know quite enough about your situation," Professor Brewster said.

"That's not it," Kevin insisted. "There has been another message! A new set of coordinates. The aliens said—"

"That's enough," Professor Brewster said. "We all put enough time and effort into chasing this charade, without trying to revive it. I'm going to hang up now, Kevin. If you contact this facility again, I will be passing the details of it along to the police."

He hung up, just as firmly as the receptionist had.

Kevin stood there, trying to work out what to do next. He didn't have any other phone numbers to try, unless he was going to attempt to call a journalist or the White House or something, and in both those cases, he suspected that he would get pretty much the same response that he'd just had. He could go home and try to talk to the journalists there, or he could wait for his mother, but both of those options risked him being ignored, and—

"So," Luna said, interrupting his thought process, "how are we getting to SETI?"

"What?" Kevin said.

"It's the best option we have," Luna said. "If we go to them, they'll see that you're serious, and they'll be able to persuade NASA to move their telescopes. Dr. Levin always seemed far nicer than that Professor Brewster anyway."

When she put it like that, she managed to make it sound so utterly logical that there was no arguing with it. Luna had a way of doing that kind of thing that was kind of terrifying, in its way. Even so, Kevin thought that he should at least try.

"My mom will kill me if I do something like that," he pointed out.

"Your mom loves you too much for that," Luna said. "Anyway, she's going to ground you forever for sneaking out as it is. You might as well save the world while you're in trouble already."

"*You* don't have to get into trouble though," Kevin pointed out. "Your parents will be mad if you just go off to San Francisco."

"You think I'm letting you do this alone?" Luna demanded. "You think I'm letting you get all the credit for finding the aliens again? You think I'm letting you have all the *fun*?"

"I'm not sure that it will be exactly fun," Kevin said.

Luna was already shaking her head. "You got to go to the jungle without me, but you're not leaving me behind for this part, Kevin."

CHAPTER TWENTY ONE

They bought bus tickets to San Francisco from a clerk who eyed them suspiciously. Kevin wasn't sure if it was because the man recognized him from the news, or because he thought they were probably runaways, or both. They still managed to buy tickets though, and snagged two seats toward the back of a bus that rattled along half full in the direction of the city. They huddled in them, and Kevin found himself grateful that Luna was there. He wasn't sure he'd be able to do this without her.

The bus journey seemed to take forever, and Kevin spent most of that time trying to work out what he might be able to say that would be able to convince them that he was telling the truth. He couldn't just ask them to trust him, not after last time.

"Of course you can," Luna said when he said as much to her. "You ask them to check the location of the signal. They might not be able to work out what it means, but they'll still *hear* it."

She made it sound easy, but the truth was that it probably was their best option. So, when the bus got into the station, Kevin set off with Luna, finding a taxi that would take them in the right direction, trying to ignore the way his body was starting to shake.

"You going for the excitement there?" the cab driver asked. "You missed most of it. They stopped talking about aliens a couple of days ago."

"Maybe they'll start again," Luna said. "You never know."

The driver took them as far as the entrance to SETI. There weren't the people camped out here that there were with the NASA facility, and Kevin was happy about that. It meant that he could simply walk in without people spotting him, or grabbing him, or—

"You?" the receptionist said almost as soon as he stepped through the door. "Didn't you get the message when I hung up on you? You've caused so much trouble here already. Get out before I call security."

Before, it had been Kevin's mother who had gotten into a shouting match with the receptionist. Now Luna started forward, obviously spoiling for an argument.

"It's okay," Dr. Levin said, stepping out into the lobby. "I've got this. Kevin, what are you doing here?"

"He's *trying* to get through to you," Luna said, the irritation easy to hear in her voice. "But apparently people who have already *betrayed* him aren't willing to listen."

"Hello, Luna," Dr. Levin said. "Do your parents know the two of you are here? You really shouldn't be here."

"There has been another message," Kevin said, guessing that they didn't have a lot of time. He didn't feel as though he had a lot of time right then. Maybe it was the effort of coming all that way, but Kevin could feel the pressure in his head building, along with a dizziness that made the world swim. He pushed it back. This was important.

"Kevin," Dr. Levin said, "we all know by now that the messages aren't real. Even if you think they are, you need to stop this."

"How did I know about Pioneer 11?" Kevin demanded. He'd had a whole bus ride in which to think about what he was going to say, and how he could convince Dr. Levin. "How did I know where the first signal would be? You saw me do that with your own eyes, Dr. Levin."

The scientist started to shake her head. "That doesn't matter."

"It does," Kevin insisted. "If you don't believe the evidence in front of you, then what's science *for*?" He paused. "If you can explain it away, just tell me. Tell me how I'm doing it, and I'll turn around and go, but I think that you can't, and you can't, because this is real, and *there's another message*."

He would have said more then, but he couldn't hold back the sudden pressure in his head.

Suddenly, he collapsed.

*

Blackness claimed Kevin. For once, there were no visions, no messages, and no signs of anything.

Just emptiness

He woke to harsh light, blinking, trying to figure out where he was.

Luna and Dr. Levin were looking down at him.

"Kevin, are you all right?" Luna asked.

"We should get you some medical attention," Dr. Levin said.

"No," Kevin managed to say, and for a moment, even he wasn't sure which question he was answering. "No more doctors. Don't call my mom. We have to listen to the signal."

134

He realized he had collapsed. He was lying on the floor, in the spot he had been standing just moments before.

He heard Dr. Levin sigh. He wasn't sure what he would do if she threw him out. Put the information on the Internet, maybe? Send it directly to some other observatory in the hope that they would do something with the information? Probably, he would be in too much trouble with his mother for that by then. He just had to stand there and hope.

He saw her eyeing him with more compassion than she had before; he suspected his collapse had shifted something within her.

"Okay," Dr. Levin said, "okay, I'll admit, I've been thinking about everything from when you first came here. Unless you somehow managed to take control of all of NASA's systems... No, it just doesn't work. But that means..."

"It means you believe me," Kevin said.

Dr. Levin nodded. "Yes, I believe you. I don't want to, but I can't see any other way. What's this message of yours?"

"Coordinates," Kevin said. "Like the last time we had to change the telescope's alignment, only different. They want us to focus on a different place."

"For messages coming from a different patch of sky?" Dr. Levin asked. Kevin heard her sigh. "You know that no one will move a telescope just on my word, right? Not after..."

"After everything I did?" Kevin guessed.

Dr. Levin nodded.

"There must be someone," Luna insisted, beside them. "Professor Brewster doesn't have to know. Or we could find a way to hack in."

It was surprising, sometimes, just how little respect for rules Luna could have. To Kevin's surprise, Dr. Levin seemed to be taking her suggestion seriously.

"Hacking NASA is hard," she said. "To do that, we'd need someone who..."

Then her eyes brightened with realization.

"Of course," she said to herself. "Phil."

Kevin nodded at the mention of the scientist's name. "Do you think... do you think he would help?"

"He might," Dr. Levin said. "He's our best shot, at least."

She and Luna helped Kevin to stand. It took an effort, but he was going to see this through.

"I can't believe that I'm doing this again," she said, "but I guess... I guess we need to take a trip to NASA."

CHAPTER TWENTY TWO

They drove over to the NASA facility in Dr. Levin's car. As the three of them drove up, there were still some people waiting outside, but fewer than there had been. They made for the gates in Dr. Levin's car. There was a security guard there, standing behind a low barrier.

"This could be tricky," Dr. Levin said. "I haven't been back since this happened."

She drove up and the guard there held up a hand.

"Can't come in here," he said, holding up a hand. "If I've told one of you, I must have told a… Dr. Levin, what are you doing here? You're not on the list for today."

"We need to get in, Neil," she said. "I need to talk to Phil."

"We?" the guard said. He looked back at the car. "Wait, isn't that…"

Kevin didn't shy away from the guard's look. Right then, it was their only hope.

"You? You aren't supposed to be here. They said—"

"They probably said all kinds of things," Dr. Levin said, "but we do need to get in. Please."

"I'm sorry, Dr. Levin," the security guard said. "But I just can't let you in like this, especially not if you're bringing *him* here."

Kevin looked across to Luna, who nodded.

"Please, Neil, this is vital," Dr. Levin said.

"I'm sorry, you need to turn your car around and… Hey!"

Kevin and Luna burst from the car practically simultaneously,

Kevin darted past him at almost the same time that Luna did. The man couldn't make a grab for both of them at once, and so they managed to slip past the barrier, running for the doors to the facility even as the security guard turned to run after them, his efforts hampered by a few of the people who had come there to protest, and who had clearly decided to follow and see what was happening.

Kevin ran forward, sprinting for the door. He and Luna were both quicker than the man was, and they made it to the doors before the guard had covered half the space. That would probably have meant much more if the doors hadn't been locked. Kevin pounded on them, but he didn't have the security clearance to get through them, had *never* had the clearance to get through them, and now the guard was bearing down on them.

"You're *both* going *straight* to the police!" he promised as he closed in.

Then the doors to the facility opened, and both Kevin and Luna stumbled inside a step ahead of the guard. The door slammed to shut him out, and Kevin looked up at the figure who had opened the door.

"Ted?" He was the last person Kevin had been expecting there, but probably also the best person they could have run into. "You're still here?"

Ted nodded. "I had to stay around to answer some questions about all this. But never mind that. What are you doing here, Kevin?" He looked over to Luna. "You're *both* here?"

"There's been another message," Kevin said.

Where the others had hung up or looked at him like he was mad, Ted gave him a serious look. "You're sure?"

Kevin nodded. "We need someone who can realign the telescope. There's another set of coordinates."

Ted watched as Dr. Levin came up, able to get through now that Ted had gotten the guard to back off. "You were coming to check?"

Dr. Levin nodded. "I was hoping that Phil might be willing to realign things quietly. The trick is getting there."

"I can handle that," Ted said. "I'm just supposed to be here to wrap things up, but I still have full access."

He took out a keycard, letting them into the building. Some of the people in the lobby stared at them as they came in, but no one said anything. Kevin guessed that had a lot to do with Ted's presence and that of Dr. Levin.

"We should move quickly," Ted said. "Someone will tell Professor Brewster that you're here soon enough."

"Just so long as we have the new messages by then," Dr. Levin said.

She led the way down toward Phil's office, with Kevin, Luna, and Ted following along behind. Kevin saw the looks some of the people gave him, heard the muttering as he passed. They hadn't forgotten what had happened before. Kevin just hoped that Phil would be willing to help.

Dr. Levin knocked on the researcher's door, and Kevin watched his face as he saw them there. It moved from recognition to surprise, and then to a kind of worried understanding.

"No," he said, holding up his hands. "Whatever it is, no."

"We haven't even asked you anything yet," Dr. Levin pointed out.

137

"But you will," Phil said, "and Professor Brewster will hear about it, and—"

"Do you care what David says?" Dr. Levin countered.

Phil shrugged, then sighed. "What do you need?"

"We need you to point the telescopes at some new coordinates," Kevin said, answering for them. "I got another message."

"You want me to… do you know what you're asking?" Phil said.

"Look at it this way," Dr. Levin pointed out. "If you do this, you'll get to be the guy who proved that Kevin was right all along."

Phil swallowed, then nodded. "Okay, but we have to do this quietly. Come on."

He led them through the facility now, taking them down to a lab space equipped with monitors and screens. A few taps on the keyboard from Phil, and it started to show the data from one of the telescope arrays.

"Okay," he said, "it looks like we're set up here. We just… oh, there goes my career."

Kevin looked round. Through the doors of the lab space, he could see Professor Brewster approaching, a thunderous expression on his face.

"What are they doing here?" he demanded as he advanced. "Stop what you're doing at once!"

Kevin guessed that it had been inevitable that someone would tell him that they were here. He'd just thought maybe they would get a little more time before it happened.

"Looks like we're done," Phil said.

"Not if we do this quickly," Kevin replied.

"Not even that quickly," Luna said. She ran over to the door, shutting it and wedging a chair under the handle. "What?" she demanded as the others looked at her. "It's just the obvious thing to do."

"Only to you," Kevin said with a smile.

Outside, Professor Brewster hammered on the glass door. "Open this at once! I shall call security! Anybody assisting that boy will be treated as a criminal!"

Kevin looked over to Phil. Without him, they wouldn't be able to realign the telescope, so if he decided not to do this…

"Okay," he said. "What are the coordinates?"

Kevin breathed a sigh of relief and recited from memory. As with the first set of numbers, these felt almost burned into him, there when he shut his eyes so that it was almost more like reading them than remembering.

"You're sure?" Phil asked.

Kevin nodded, opening his eyes. There were more people outside the door now, gathering around to watch what was happening, or trying to help Professor Brewster get in there.

"Here we go then," Phil said. He pressed another button, and Kevin saw the numbers on the screen shift as the focus of the radio telescope started to change. They shifted little by little, the numbers getting closer to the ones he saw, and closer, until...

The moment they matched, a signal came through, clear and strong. Sounds started to come from the system. They had a familiar feel to them, but at the same time they seemed different from some of the ones Kevin had translated. Less precise and mechanical, more flowing.

Even so, he found himself translating them automatically.

"If you are receiving this, beware," he translated. "You are in grave danger. The last messages you received were a trick."

Kevin could hear Professor Brewster continuing to hammer on the door, but he kept listening, and now the translation flowed from him.

"Their transmissions were a lie, designed to make you open the capsule. It is no time capsule. It is a weapon. It has destroyed us completely. This is our final transmission, to warn others not to make the same mistake we did."

Kevin frowned, not sure if he was translating it right, but the message wasn't done.

Brewster and his team burst through the door.

"What is the meaning of this?" he demanded—but stopped short as he listened, too.

"Do not make the mistakes we did. Do not open what they send to you."

The message stopped, then repeated, as if it were being sent on some kind of loop.

"Someone wanted to make sure that we heard it," Luna said.

Kevin nodded, trying to make sense of it. He looked over to the adults.

"Where is the rock?" Brewster asked.

"Downstairs—Lab 3b."

"Get them on the phone!" Ted yelled. "NOW!"

CHAPTER TWENTY THREE

Kevin ran, trying to keep up with Dr. Levin, Luna, and Ted as they hurried through the NASA institute, trying to get to the space where the rock was being kept. He could see the shocked looks on the faces of the scientists they raced past, some of them obviously recognizing him, others probably just surprised that anyone would run that fast through a serious scientific facility.

Dr. Levin held out a set of keys to Kevin.

"If this goes wrong," she said as she ran, "if there's something you can't contain, there's a secure space below the facility, on the sub-basement level. One of these keys provides access to the bunker network, if it isn't locked down. Use this, and the elevator should take you straight there."

"Where is the rock from the expedition being held?" Ted called out to a group of scientists as they passed.

"Research Lab 3b," one of them said. "Why? Is there something—"

They were already sprinting past, trying to make it there in time. They paused at security doors, but those only slowed them down a little, opening for Ted's security card with green lights and reassuring whooshes of air.

Kevin could hear Professor Brewster yelling behind them, but he didn't slow.

They went deep into the bowels of the building, past laboratories that Kevin had seen while Phil had been showing him around. He passed the lasers and the growing labs, the things that promised to give humanity a chance to survive and thrive if they ever got to another world, and the things that carried the promise of making this one a better place. Right then, the only thing that mattered was the threat of what might happen if they didn't make sure that the rock was contained.

They paused at a set of signs, then ran on again, down a set of stairs and into a part of the building where the only light was artificial. It felt sterile to Kevin, unwelcoming compared to the rest of the place. The scientists they passed were mostly in clean suits or lab coats, obviously trying to keep from contaminating experiments.

When they came to the lab, Kevin had to admit that it *looked* like a secure space. It had toughened glass walls on three sides, while the fourth backed onto the outer wall of the building. The rock sat in the middle of it, displayed on a table like an Easter egg that had been cracked in half. Three scientists stood around it in white plastic clean suits. Two were wearing masks, while one didn't seem to have bothered, since he was away from the rock, working with a microscope.

The glass was thick, but Kevin could still hear what they were saying while Ted worked at the lock, trying to get in.

"These samples are still interesting," the scientist said. "Even if it's not anything that we were promised."

"Don't let Brewster hear you saying that," another replied. "As far as he's concerned, the sooner we can declare that rock worthless and get rid of it, the better."

"Well, he might have to wait, this is…"

"What?" the third scientist asked. "And will you put a mask on? It's protocol."

Kevin saw the moment when vapor started to rise from the surface of the rock. It was almost clear, and he could have mistaken it for steam rising due to some temperature change in the rock, but somehow, he knew it wasn't.

"That keeps happening," one of the scientists said.

Kevin banged his hand against the glass, while Ted kept working on the lock.

"It's a code as well as a card," he said. "I guess it's because it's a sealed room."

"You need to get out of there," Kevin called. "You're all in danger."

They turned toward him as he continued to bang his hand on the glass, obviously not sure why he was there, or what they should do. The two with the facemasks looked puzzled. The one without…

The eyes of the one who wasn't wearing a mask suddenly changed, the pupils turning from black to white, seeming almost to shine. He stared at Kevin, and there was a kind of recognition there that hadn't been present before. There was a kind of hostility to that look that filled Kevin with fear.

It was intelligent, and dangerous.

And anything but human.

CHAPTER TWENTY FOUR

"Get back from him!" Kevin yelled. "There's something wrong with him."

The scientist spun to the other two and made a grab for them, pulling their masks away before they realized what was happening. Kevin wanted to call out a warning, but it looked as though it was already too late. He saw the scientists' eyes shift, their pupils turning as white as the others'.

Kevin backed away from the glass, looking across to Luna. She looked just as frightened as he felt right then, which probably wasn't a good sign. Luna didn't get scared.

Ted looked as though he was trying to work out what to do too, and that was almost as frightening. Kevin was used to him having all the answers. He had a phone out and was making a call.

"We have a level four breach," he said into it. "I'm working to contain it, but you need to start emergency protocols, *now*."

There was a panel on the wall. Ted pulled it open, tapping a series of numbers into a keypad. He pressed a button, and lights started to flash red along all of the corridors, while a computerized voice sounded through speakers.

"Emergency, Emergency. Containment in progress."

Metal shutters slid down the sides of all the labs on that level, effectively turning them into giant metal boxes from which nothing could escape. Kevin heard a roar of frustration from inside the lab, and he dared to breathe a sigh of relief.

"Have we done it?" he asked. "Have we stopped them?"

"I hope so," Ted said. Despite that, he went to a storage locker, pulling out the kind of filtration masks that the scientists had been wearing. He passed one each to Luna and Kevin, then took another for himself.

"What is going on here? Why is this whole space shut off?"

Kevin turned to see Professor Brewster approaching, along with Dr. Levin and at least a dozen others. A security guard had a hold of Dr. Levin's elbow, looking apologetic about it, but not letting go.

"You've gone too far," the facility's director said, pointing a finger in their direction. "You had no *right* to do this."

"You're lucky we did," Luna said, before either Kevin or Ted could say anything, "because you'd be surrounded by aliens by now if we hadn't."

"Aliens," Professor Brewster said with a note of contempt. "Haven't we heard enough of this nonsense?"

"Oh, it's a long way from being nonsense," Ted said. "I've seen it."

"It's true," Kevin said. "They can take over people's bodies. A gas came out of the rock we found, and it took over the scientists there."

Professor Brewster shook his head. "There are many gases that can produce erratic behavior, and that's if anything happened at all. We only have your word for it."

"*My* word," Ted said, in a tone that dared the other man to contradict it.

That was when the knocking sounded.

"Knocking" wasn't quite the right word for it. That made it sound almost polite, even delicate, but the sound that reverberated in Kevin's ears was of something smashing, hard, against the walls of the room.

"There are people locked in there?" Professor Brewster demanded.

"The aliens are controlling them," Kevin said. "Their pupils turned white when it happened."

"Probably just a trick of chemical reaction," Professor Brewster insisted. "Either way, this foolishness has gone on long enough. I'm going to release my people, call security down here, and have all of you removed from this facility."

He started for the security panel that Ted had used, and Kevin saw the soldier pull out a gun.

"I will shoot anyone who touches those controls," Ted promised.

That shocked Kevin a little. He didn't want anyone getting shot because of this. Although, if it had to be someone from there, Professor Brewster was probably top of the list. The scientist turned back toward them, his hands raised.

"You wouldn't dare!" he said. From inside the steel box of the shutters, the banging resumed.

"Um... I think he might," Kevin replied. "Professor Brewster, we can't let them out of that room. We have to stop the aliens while we can."

"There aren't any aliens!" Professor Brewster insisted. "You've imprisoned my people on a delusion, and..."

The knocking stopped, and the suddenness with which it did so made even the facility's director pause. Something clicked and whirred, then the lights in the corridor stopped flashing their dull red, and the steel shutters started to rise.

"That doesn't look good," Luna said.

That was an understatement. The shutters rose, and Kevin saw the scientists standing there passively, looking calm as they waited for the chance to be free. Kevin guessed it made sense that aliens would be able to hack a computer. After all, they had technology that had sent them halfway across a galaxy. Compared to that, a computer probably wasn't very complicated.

"You see," Professor Brewster said. "There are no aliens, just three perfectly normal—"

The scientists opened their mouths, shrieking in unison, a noise that sounded more insect-like than human, more alien than either. Kevin saw the shock on the expressions of the scientists around him as they realized that these weren't their colleagues anymore.

"Look at their eyes," one of the researchers said.

Kevin looked over to Ted. "We're safe out here, right?"

"As long as they can't get through the glass," Ted said. "All of you, you need facemasks. If any of that vapor gets out, you're all in danger."

Professor Brewster looked as though he was trying to gather himself to say that there was no problem, that it was all fine, but he seemed to be having trouble doing it. He was still trying to say it when the scientists the aliens controlled picked up a metal chair and started to hammer at the glass with it like a battering ram, all three of them working in concert as the sound of it boomed around the facility.

Cracks started to appear on the glass. Kevin saw them spread like a spider's web over the surface, rippling out and joining with every blow. Ted leveled his gun at the scientists, but it didn't make them stop, or even slow.

The glass broke, and they charged out. Kevin heard Ted's gun go off, but it didn't seem to make any difference. Kevin saw those scientists who weren't wearing masks freeze in place, gasping as they grabbed at their throats, then straightening up. One lunged at a neighbor who was masked, ripping it away and then breathing out a clear mist that filled the space in front of them. In moments, that scientist was converted too.

One grabbed Kevin, ripping away the mask he wore. Kevin tried to hold his breath, tried to pull away, but there was no way to do it. A foul-smelling vapor stole over him…

144

…and nothing happened.

Luna smashed into the side of the scientist holding Kevin. She was small, but she'd had plenty of experience hitting people bigger than herself, and it was at least enough to make the scientist loosen his grip.

"Run!" Ted yelled. "Get to the bunker!"

He started firing his gun into the melee. It didn't stop the scientists. Whatever was controlling them didn't seem to care about human things like pain, or the damage being done to the bodies they held in their grasp. As Kevin watched, three scientists grabbed hold of Ted, dragging him down.

Kevin wanted to help Ted, wanted to dart forward and pull him out of the mess, but there was no way to do it, no way to even begin to help. The most that he could do was grab Luna's arm and pull her clear, the two of them running from the advancing scientists.

Looking back, Kevin saw them transforming one by one. He saw Dr. Levin gasp, clutching at her throat as the gas got into her, then straighten up in a way that was far too calm, far too still.

He saw Professor Brewster shift in a matter of moments, the gas overwhelming him.

Some part of him thought that Ted would somehow fight it off, that he would break clear and come to help them. Kevin let out a heartbroken cry as he saw the soldier go still, then stand, joining in the others as they chased them.

They hurried together down the facility's corridors, more and more scientists following after them with a determination that wasn't human anymore, wasn't even close to it. Looking back, Kevin could see Ted, Dr. Levin, and Professor Brewster, just as alien as all the rest. A part of him wanted to just collapse to his knees, broken by the shock of it. Only Luna's presence beside him kept him running.

"This way," Luna said, pulling him down a side corridor, then off through a series of rooms holding scientific equipment. They ducked down behind a series of large microscopes, holding still while, beyond the doors, alien-possessed scientists advanced through the facility, almost mindlessly, grabbing hold of anyone they encountered to convert them.

Luna knelt, and she stared at Kevin. "Let me look in your eyes."

Kevin knew what he had to be looking for. "I'm not an alien."

"No, you're not, but you should be. I don't know how you aren't." She shook her head. "What do we do?"

She seemed to take it for granted that there would be something they could do. Kevin didn't. If his disease had taught him anything, it was that there were some things it was impossible to do anything about.

"Ted said to get to the bunker," Kevin said.

Luna nodded. "Do you have the key?"

Kevin held it up.

"Okay," she said. "Let's go."

Kevin led the way, creeping through the scientific equipment, heading in the direction of the elevators. Every so often they would stop, and both Kevin and Luna would freeze in place, waiting while scientists moved past. There weren't many now. Kevin guessed that they were probably moving through the rest of the facility, converting people as they went. It was a little like those days when they crept into places they shouldn't be, and had to keep out of sight of adults, only really, it was nothing like that. They weren't just going to be given a stern warning or told to move on if they were caught.

The elevators lay ahead, just beyond a room full of plants set out for testing. In front of them, half a dozen of the scientists stood waiting, as if knowing that the two of them would be going that way.

They probably *did* know, Kevin realized. From what had happened in the lab, it looked as though they had access to the thoughts and memories of the people they controlled, so why wouldn't they know about the bunker?

"What do we do?" Luna asked.

Kevin tried to think. "We need a distraction."

He picked up one of the plants, considering its ceramic pot. He moved to the door of the room furthest from the elevator, picking a direction. Then he set the plant's container rolling, as hard as he could, hurrying back to Luna just in time for a crash to sound in the distance.

The alien-controlled scientists turned toward the sound, then hurried forward in that awful, synchronized silence that they had.

"Now," Kevin said, and he and Luna scurried toward the elevators. There was a lock set by them at about chest level.

"Quick," Luna said, "use the key."

Kevin pushed it into a lock by the elevators, and a green light shone. The elevator doors rolled open with agonizing slowness. How long would it be before the aliens spotted what had made the sound and worked out that they had been tricked? How long before they came back for the two of them?

An inhuman sound not far away suggested that it wouldn't be long.

"Inside," Luna said, and they both stumbled back into the elevator car.

There was another keyhole inside the elevator, along with a button at the bottom of the controls labeled simply "Bunker." There were other buttons too, for the various levels of the facility, for its lobby and its parking garage. Kevin stood there, considering them.

"What are you waiting for?" Luna asked. "You heard Ted, we need to get to the bunker."

Kevin nodded. He'd heard. There was only one problem.

"What happens to our parents?" he asked.

He saw Luna's eyes widen.

Outside, he saw aliens coming around the corner, all of them moving toward the elevators with perfect synchronization.

"If we go to the bunker, who'll save our parents?" Kevin asked. He couldn't just abandon his mother to become an alien. He couldn't.

So as the alien-controlled scientists started to rush forward, Kevin pressed the only button he could.

CHAPTER TWENTY FIVE

Kevin could only stand there as the elevator headed up, toward the lobby. The seconds seemed to stretch out, and with every one that passed he could imagine the scientists running through the building, grabbing more people and breathing the vapor on them, or just waiting while it spread through the building, maybe beyond.

The elevator rumbled up, the lights flickering in a way that suggested something was happening elsewhere in the building; something violent.

"Do you think they'll be able to stop this?" Luna asked. She actually sounded scared. As scared as Kevin felt, right then.

"I don't know," he admitted, and not knowing was one of the worst parts of it. He had no idea what was going to happen, or if this could be stopped, or how.

Slowly, the elevator ground to a halt, the doors opening to reveal the lobby beyond. Kevin and Luna crept into it silently, not daring to take their masks off as they hurried through it.

One look at the floor told Kevin that it was the right thing. He could see vapor trailing along it like mist on a cold morning, pouring out from under the doors and spreading, caught by the breeze outside. He couldn't see it as it touched the protesters, but he could see the effects as they breathed it, could see them going still one by one, staring up as if waiting for something.

"No," Luna said, and Kevin could hear the horror in her voice. "No, it can't be spreading this quickly."

Kevin swallowed back his own fear. How could the vapor be doing so much, so fast? But he knew the answer to that: it had been designed to all along, and that was the most terrifying thought of all, because it meant that the people outside were just the start.

Kevin couldn't work out how they were going to get past them, but it seemed that Luna had an idea. She was already leading the way out of the institute, heading for the parking lot there.

"What are you doing?" Kevin asked her.

"If we're going to get home in time, we can't take the bus," Luna said. "We need a car."

"So you're going to steal one?" Kevin asked. "Can you even drive?"

It seemed inconceivable to him that anyone their age might be able to, but Luna seemed pretty confident.

148

"Not steal, borrow," Luna said. "And yes, I can drive. Probably. One of my cousins let me drive his truck once. It's not *that* hard."

They went into the parking lot, staring at all the cars there. Kevin wasn't sure what it would take to steal one of them, or how long it would take to do it. He wasn't sure that they had a lot of time. Already, he could see some of those outside the facility's fence turning toward them.

"Um... Luna?" he said. "I think we need to hurry."

"There!" she said, pointing. Kevin recognized Dr. Levin's compact city car immediately. "She gave you all her keys, right?"

"I'm not sure," Kevin said. He took them out. "She gave me the one to the elevator, but..." One stood out immediately. "Does this one look like a car key?"

"It does," Luna said. She snatched it from his hand, moving to the car and opening the doors. Glancing back, Kevin could see the people the aliens controlled advancing now, moving toward them and toward the facility in a single, synchronized group.

Kevin dove into the car, where Luna was already working with the key, trying to make the thing start.

"I thought you knew what you were doing," he said.

"This is different from my cousin's truck," she replied. "Give me a minute."

Kevin looked over the dashboard at the advancing horde of scientists. "I'm not sure that we *have* a minute."

"Wait, I think I've got it!" The engine didn't exactly roar to life, given how small the car was, but it started. Luna threw it into gear, and they lurched forward, crunching it against the car in front.

"Other way," Kevin said.

"Do you want to drive?" Luna shot back. She managed to get it into reverse, backing out of the parking space with another scrape of metal on metal. She put the car back into drive and they set off for the gate.

A protester flung himself in front of the car, bouncing off the hood and then rising to his feet, apparently unharmed. Kevin had seen Ted shoot the controlled scientists without it stopping them though, so he doubted the car had done much. Another flung itself onto the hood, holding on tight, white-pupiled eyes staring straight at them.

"Get it off! Get it off!" Luna yelled.

Kevin wasn't sure how he was supposed to do that, but he did his best. Rolling down the window on his side, he leaned out, wrenching at the protestor's grip. He yanked, and the protestor fell clear, tumbling to the concrete.

They were clear then, driving away through the NASA compound, heading for the highway while controlled people trailed after them. The small car burst out onto the roads, and Kevin looked around, hoping that he would see people just going about their business, half hoping that there would be cops there who would stop them for driving so erratically, so that they could warn people about what was happening.

Instead, people stood by the sides of the road, perfectly still as they stared at the sky.

"The vapor's spreading," Kevin said.

Luna nodded. "We have to get to our parents. Now."

They barreled down the road. Kevin could see Luna's knuckles were white on the steering wheel as she drove, her face set with concentration. Despite that, they wove and braked as she struggled to get used to it. If there had been other people driving there, Kevin had no doubt that they would have crashed within the first mile. Instead, the only other cars on the roads were stationary ones, abandoned at the sides, or occasionally just in the middle of the highway while their owners got out to stare at the sky.

This was his fault. If he'd never said anything about what he'd seen, if he'd never led people to the rock, then this wouldn't have happened. There wouldn't be people standing there as blankly as mannequins, the effect spreading...

His mother. She would be out there, not knowing what was happening. Not knowing what to do. Would she be safe? What if she was like them here? No, Kevin couldn't stand that thought. Kevin got his phone out, trying to call his mother to warn her. He wasn't surprised to find a half dozen missed calls from her, all the messages wanting to know where he was. He called her back.

"Kevin?" she said as she picked up. "Kevin, where are you? Where have you been? You weren't home when I got back. I've been going out of my mind!"

Kevin sighed with relief because, by the sound of it, his mother was still very much occupying her own mind.

"Mom, I'm with Luna," he said.

"Luna? What are you two doing? Where are you? There's stuff on TV... They're saying all kinds of things."

"It's hard to explain, Mom," Kevin said. "We went to the NASA institute to warn people that the aliens had tricked us, but we were too late."

"The aliens?" Kevin's mother said. "Kevin, you went all that way? It wasn't safe, and—"

"Mom," Kevin said, "you have to listen to me. There was a kind of gas or something inside the rock. It changes people, it lets the aliens control them. You have to find a facemask, or a place that isn't open to the air."

"Kevin," his mother said. "This really doesn't sound—"

"I'm not crazy, Mom," Kevin insisted, before his mother could finish it. "I'm not. Just look at the TV. If you don't believe me, Luna will tell you."

He held out the phone for Luna to speak. He wasn't sure if it was such a good idea, distracting her like that, but he needed to do *something* to try to keep his mother safe.

"Ms. McKenzie, it's all true," Luna said. "You need to listen to me. I saw it. I saw the scientists change... Yes, I know it sounds crazy, but I swear it's true. We're coming to get you now."

She jerked the wheel sharply to avoid another car and Kevin pulled the phone away.

"Mom? We'll be there as soon as we can. If anyone tries to get in, look at their eyes. If their pupils are white, don't let them in. Even us. And Mom? I love you."

It probably wasn't a cool thing to say, but right then, Kevin didn't care. He wanted his mother to know.

"I love you too," his mother said. "Whatever this is, we'll find a way to sort it all out."

Kevin wasn't so sure it would be that easy. He hung up, calling Luna's parents next since there was no way she would be able to do it without either stopping or crashing. He called her mom, then her dad, hearing the phone go through to voicemail each time.

"No answer," he said.

Luna looked over at him. "Do you think that means—"

"Look out!" Kevin said, grabbing the wheel to pull them away from a knot of people who stepped onto the road to look at the sky. Their car skidded briefly, scraping along the side of the road before continuing on.

Luna fastened her grip on the wheel again, not saying anything now as she drove, faster and faster as her confidence grew. Kevin suspected that she should probably slow down a little, but he wasn't going to be the one to tell her that right then, especially not when they still needed to get to his own mother.

It seemed to take forever before they pulled into Walnut Creek, and everything there seemed too quiet; eerily so. As Luna pulled the car up in front of Kevin's house, it occurred to him that she shouldn't have been able to. They should have been surrounded by reporters, all eager to photograph him doing something he shouldn't be doing.

Instead, the street was empty.

"Where are they all?" Kevin wondered aloud.

"Do you *want* to be pestered by reporters?" Luna countered. "Probably they're off covering everything that's happening, or they decided to take cover. I would."

"We *will*," Kevin promised. Just as soon as they'd gotten their parents. "My mom should have seen us pull up."

He went from the car over to the house, ringing the doorbell, and then banging on the door.

"Mom," he shouted, "it's not a reporter. It's me, Kevin."

He waited there for several seconds, not sure if the quiet was because his mother was hiding, or because it meant something more sinister. He dared to breathe a sigh of relief when he heard the click of the latch and the door started to open.

"Mom!" Kevin said, throwing his arms wide to hug her, not caring that it was an uncool thing to do. She stood there in front of him, smiling with her own arms open, looking safe, looking happy…

…Then Kevin saw her eyes, blank white and staring, and realized that his mother was grabbing, not hugging.

It was too late, he realized, a yawning pit opening up in his stomach.

The aliens had her.

CHAPTER TWENTY SIX

For a moment, Kevin just stood there, paralyzed by the grief he felt. He could feel tears starting to roll down his cheeks. They'd taken over his mom. They'd controlled her, like they'd controlled so many other people, but this was different, because it was his mom, not someone else. He felt angry, and sad, and guilty, all at once. He'd done this. He'd told them where to find the rock. He'd—

"Kevin, run!" Luna said, jerking him back from his mom.

He managed to jump back out of his mother's grip, but she lurched forward after the two of them, breathing out the vapor that might convert them.

More figures came from the buildings all around, pouring from them in a way that said they'd been waiting for Kevin and Luna to arrive just so that they could do it. Some of them looked like reporters, with camera gear still strapped to them as they came for them. Kevin could see worse than that. Luna's parents stood there, as blank-eyed and unseeing as the rest. The most terrifying thing was how normal they looked as they did it.

It was enough to send Kevin scrambling for the car. He made it as Luna took her place in the driver's spot.

"Drive!" he yelled to Luna as he managed to fall into the passenger's seat.

"Those... those are my parents," Luna said, and despite her mask Kevin could see how pale her features were then, how upset she was.

"I know, Luna, but if we don't get out of here, we're going to end up like them, or worse."

Luna looked over at him and Kevin could see the tears. Even so, Luna nodded, stepping on the gas pedal so the car lurched forward. Reporters bounced off the hood. Kevin was just grateful that it wasn't Luna's parents, even if the reporters got straight back up again.

They kept going more than a mile before they stopped, in the middle of a deserted lot where there was no sign of anyone. Luna turned off the engine and cried. Right then, Kevin knew how she felt. His mother was gone, taken by the aliens just like that. He'd tried to warn her. Had she not believed him, opened the door to someone? Had it just been too late?

Kevin didn't know. Right then, it didn't matter. His mom was gone, changed, and so were Luna's parents. So was *every* adult they'd been able to trust. Dr. Levin. Ted. All of them were gone. The world felt like a much bigger, scarier place without them there to help.

He felt empty right then, in a way that made all the things he'd felt when he'd learned that he was going to die seem like nothing. Was this what his mother had felt, hearing that he was dying? This sense of loss?

"Promise me something," Luna said between the tears. "Promise me that you won't let me be like that."

"We're safe," Kevin said. Even to himself, he didn't sound convincing. "We have masks."

"A mask won't stop them if they pull it away and breathe that *stuff* on me," Luna said. She sounded angry now. Not angry at Kevin; angry at the world. "It won't keep me from being like them. So promise me you won't let me be like them."

"How can I—" Kevin began.

"You can kill me," Luna said. The tears in her eyes made them glisten. "I don't want to be some mindless thing, trapped in my own body. If I end up like that, I want you to kill me. Say you'll do it, Kevin."

Kevin couldn't say it. He couldn't promise to kill Luna. How could anyone promise that? The best he could do was to stay silent while Luna cried, his hand on her shoulder in silent support.

"Where do we go, Kevin?" Luna asked. She sounded as though she was choking back her sobs now. "Where *can* we go? What can we do? What if… what if *everyone's* like this?"

Kevin wasn't sure he had an answer to that.

"We need to get somewhere safe," he said. "Ted wanted us to do that."

"He wanted us to get to the bunker," Luna said. "We can't go there now, can we?"

Kevin thought about all the scientists who would be in the way, who had come pouring out after them. He shook his head.

"No. We wouldn't get through."

"Where then?" Luna said. "We have to go somewhere. We can't take the masks off unless we do."

Kevin wasn't so sure about that. After all, one of the scientists had grabbed his mask. "I think… I think I can," he said.

"Well, I can't," Luna shot back. "How am I supposed to eat, Kevin? Or drink anything, or—"

"We'll think of something," Kevin said, and then froze, as he realized something. "There are more bunkers."

"*More* bunkers?" Luna said. "But wouldn't they be hidden?"

"Phil told me about some of them when he was giving me the tour of the institute," Kevin said. "He even showed me a map."

Behind her mask, Luna looked hopeful. "Can you remember where they are?"

"I..."

"Try, Kevin," Luna insisted.

Kevin did his best. He could remember one for certain. "Phil said there was one in the state park up on Mount Diablo. He said something about it being a place they used to do military tests."

"You're sure?" Luna asked.

Kevin nodded. "It would be safer than being outside," Kevin said. He tried to think about what they would need, and how it would work. "We'd need supplies. Food and stuff."

In the end, they took what they needed from a gas station. They didn't have any money to pay for it, but the clerk was busy standing at the back of the store, staring up at the sky. Kevin left a note anyway, with his mother's address. It didn't feel right just stealing stuff, even with everything that was going on.

They drove on, and now Luna seemed to be getting the hang of it, because the whole journey seemed smoother. There was certainly less crashing into things, although they still had to dodge around cars that had been abandoned in the middle of the highway, the former drivers getting out to look up. There were even a couple of police cars there, and Luna slowed down almost automatically as they drove past. But the police were just as busy staring as everyone else. There was no one to get them into trouble—and no one to help them either.

"Do you think there's anything we can do to help our parents?" Luna asked after a while.

"I don't know," Kevin admitted. He'd been thinking about that almost constantly since he'd seen his mother like that. "I guess I should know."

He'd had so many messages from the aliens, but none of them had said anything about how to undo all of this. None of them had provided a cure to whatever this was, or even suggested that it could be undone. A horrible thought came to Kevin then: the aliens had burned their own world to stop this from spreading, trying to burn off the threat, and even that hadn't stopped it.

"What if there isn't a way?" Luna said. "What if everyone is stuck like that forever?"

"If there is something, we'll find it," Kevin said, although he didn't know how they could even begin to do that. He had to hope, though. He wanted to bring his mother back, and not spend the rest of his life hiding from any group of people he met.

They drove east, and kept driving. The road twisted and turned as they went up through the foothills, obscuring the mountain for a while, but soon it came back into view. They drove upward, and Kevin did his best to think where the red dot on the map had been marking the bunker. It was hard, because he'd only seen it briefly, and a lot of stuff had happened since.

"I think it's near the top," he said.

Luna nodded, and kept driving. There were fewer people out here, but even so, they were doing the same things others had been: standing by the road, staring at the sky. A few were walking back toward the city, too, as if there were something there waiting for them.

There was supposed to be a parking lot at the top of the mountain, but Luna pulled the car off the road a little way before that, hiding it in a stand of trees.

"So that it will still be here if we need it," she said. Kevin couldn't see who might be there to steal it, but even so, it sounded like a good idea. He guessed that there might be people about in the tourist areas, all controlled by the aliens now.

They took food and supplies from the car, a few cans and packets that didn't seem like enough now that they were here. They crept forward through the trees, trying not to make a sound.

"Which way to the bunker from here?" Luna asked.

"I'm not sure," Kevin admitted. "I think right at the top."

Luna nodded, and they started upward. It was hard, climbing that way, but they kept going. They were almost at the top anyway, and the prospect of safety pulled them on.

There were people near the top. Kevin could see them as he got closer. Some looked like tourists, but there were others in military uniforms, suggesting that Phil's talk of a hidden military testing site might be true. All seemed to be as still as everyone else he'd seen, as if waiting for orders. He knew that they couldn't just walk past them, though. If even one saw him, how many more would come? If there were enough, it wouldn't matter that they had a bunker to go to.

So they crept along as best they could, trying to keep as many trees as possible between them and the people there. Kevin kept his head low, trying to keep out of sight. He saw people slowly turning to stare at him through the trees, and he knew that their efforts to stay out of sight hadn't worked.

"Run!" he called to Luna.

They ran, while the group of those by the lake started forward as one, moving at no more than a walking pace, but looking as though they wouldn't stop for anything. Kevin and Luna rushed through the trees, heading deeper out of sight.

"There," Luna whispered, pointing.

Kevin sighed with relief. She was right. They'd found it.

The entrance to the bunker was camouflaged with green and gray, moss and small plants. The entrance looked like a small hollow in the ground from a distance, but closer to it, it was possible to see the steps leading down. There was a door there closed by an old-fashioned round handle, like a ship's wheel, or a safe. A keyhole sat at the center. Kevin just hoped that Phil had been right about the same keys working everywhere.

"Quickly," Luna said.

Kevin could hear the crashing behind them now of the alien-controlled people closing in. The two of them rushed for the door. Kevin set the key into the lock, and so slowly that it terrified him, the wheel started to turn.

The door came open just in time.

He and Luna dove inside, slamming it behind them and winding the locking mechanism shut. Something slammed into it from the other side, but the door held.

"Beginning decontamination procedure," an electronic voice said. Water came down in a swift burst that drenched them both like a heavy storm. Right then, Kevin didn't even mind.

"We did it," he said. "We're safe."

CHAPTER TWENTY SEVEN

To Kevin's surprise, the bunker was empty, no one left in it, despite whatever precautions must have been in place. It felt strange being trapped in there with only Luna for company.

The bunker had an operations center with screens bigger than they were. Kevin pushed a button and was relieved to see the bunker's systems let them patch into TV and the Internet, satellite images and more. There were even things that looked as though they would access military communications channels, although Kevin hadn't figured out how to work those yet.

"Is there anyone left?" Luna asked.

Kevin wasn't sure how to answer that. "There are broadcasts and things," he said, "so there must be someone."

There didn't seem to be many people, though. From the sealed off interior of the bunker, Kevin and Luna watched the world change. There was news out there on the Internet, talking about the people being transformed. It wasn't just America now, and it was spreading too fast to contain. Perhaps if people had managed to close their borders in time, they might have stopped it, but even then, what could they do about a vapor carried on the wind?

"What do you think our parents are doing now?" Luna asked.

"I don't know," Kevin admitted. It was a strange, wrenching feeling not knowing like that. Would his mother be out there with the others, just staring? Would the people like that eat or drink, remember to sleep? Or would they just stand there until they fell from exhaustion?

"There are still some people trying to show what's happening," Luna said. She showed Kevin images of a TV station where they were trying to map it all in front of what looked like a weather map, and an Internet site where someone had managed to tap into a bunch of cameras around the world.

"London, Paris, Beijing," Kevin said, reading from the captions. They were hard to tell apart, because each one showed almost the same scene, with people just standing there. Then it got worse, because on the screens, the images started to shift, showing people staring up at the sky now, coming out into the streets in hundreds, in thousands, gathering together to look up.

It took a moment to work out what they were looking *at*.

Kevin watched the screen, and he couldn't believe what he was seeing. He saw the people staring up at the sky, and he saw the shadow that started to pass over them, too sudden to be anything natural.

And too big, by far, to be anything built by human hands.

ARRIVAL
(The Invasion Chronicles—Book Two)

From #1 worldwide bestselling fantasy author Morgan Rice comes a long-anticipated science fiction series. SETI has received a signal from an alien civilization. Is there time to save the world?

"A great plot, the kind of book you will have trouble putting down at night. The ending was a cliffhanger so spectacular that you will immediately want to buy the next book just to see what happens."
–The Dallas Examiner (regarding Loved)

"Another brilliant series, immersing us in a fantasy of honor, courage, magic and faith in your destiny.....Recommended for the permanent library of all readers that love a well-written fantasy."
–Books and Movie Reviews, Roberto Mattos, re Rise of the Dragons

"A quick and easy read...you have to read what happens next and you don't want to put it down."
–FantasyOnline.net, re A Quest of Heroes

In the aftermath of SETI's receiving the signal, 13 year old Kevin realizes: he is the only one who can save the world. But is there time? What must he do?

And what do the aliens plan next?

"Action-packed …. Rice's writing is solid and the premise intriguing."
–Publishers Weekly, re A Quest of Heroes

"A superior fantasy… A recommended winner for any who enjoy epic fantasy writing fueled by powerful, believable young adult protagonists."
–Midwest Book Review, re Rise of the Dragons

"An action packed fantasy sure to please fans of Morgan Rice's previous novels, along with fans of works such as THE

INHERITANCE CYCLE by Christopher Paolini…. Fans of Young Adult Fiction will devour this latest work by Rice and beg for more."

–The Wanderer, A Literary Journal (regarding Rise of the Dragons)

Book #3 in the series will be available soon.

Also available are Morgan Rice's many series in the fantasy genre, including A QUEST OF HEROES (BOOK #1 IN THE SORCERER'S RING), a free download with over 1,300 five star reviews!

Books by Morgan Rice

THE INVASION CHRONICLES
TRANSMISSION (Book #1)
ARRIVAL (Book #2)

THE WAY OF STEEL
ONLY THE WORTHY (Book #1)

A THRONE FOR SISTERS
A THRONE FOR SISTERS (Book #1)
A COURT FOR THIEVES (Book #2)
A SONG FOR ORPHANS (Book #3)
A DIRGE FOR PRINCES (Book #4)
A JEWEL FOR ROYALS (BOOK #5)
A KISS FOR QUEENS (BOOK #6)
A CROWN FOR ASSASSINS (Book #7)

OF CROWNS AND GLORY
SLAVE, WARRIOR, QUEEN (Book #1)
ROGUE, PRISONER, PRINCESS (Book #2)
KNIGHT, HEIR, PRINCE (Book #3)
REBEL, PAWN, KING (Book #4)
SOLDIER, BROTHER, SORCERER (Book #5)
HERO, TRAITOR, DAUGHTER (Book #6)
RULER, RIVAL, EXILE (Book #7)
VICTOR, VANQUISHED, SON (Book #8)

KINGS AND SORCERERS
RISE OF THE DRAGONS (Book #1)
RISE OF THE VALIANT (Book #2)
THE WEIGHT OF HONOR (Book #3)
A FORGE OF VALOR (Book #4)
A REALM OF SHADOWS (Book #5)
NIGHT OF THE BOLD (Book #6)

THE SORCERER'S RING
A QUEST OF HEROES (Book #1)
A MARCH OF KINGS (Book #2)
A FATE OF DRAGONS (Book #3)

A CRY OF HONOR (Book #4)
A VOW OF GLORY (Book #5)
A CHARGE OF VALOR (Book #6)
A RITE OF SWORDS (Book #7)
A GRANT OF ARMS (Book #8)
A SKY OF SPELLS (Book #9)
A SEA OF SHIELDS (Book #10)
A REIGN OF STEEL (Book #11)
A LAND OF FIRE (Book #12)
A RULE OF QUEENS (Book #13)
AN OATH OF BROTHERS (Book #14)
A DREAM OF MORTALS (Book #15)
A JOUST OF KNIGHTS (Book #16)
THE GIFT OF BATTLE (Book #17)

THE SURVIVAL TRILOGY
ARENA ONE: SLAVERSUNNERS (Book #1)
ARENA TWO (Book #2)
ARENA THREE (Book #3)

VAMPIRE, FALLEN
BEFORE DAWN (Book #1)

THE VAMPIRE JOURNALS
TURNED (Book #1)
LOVED (Book #2)
BETRAYED (Book #3)
DESTINED (Book #4)
DESIRED (Book #5)
BETROTHED (Book #6)
VOWED (Book #7)
FOUND (Book #8)
RESURRECTED (Book #9)
CRAVED (Book #10)
FATED (Book #11)
OBSESSED (Book #12)

About Morgan Rice

Morgan Rice is the #1 bestselling and USA Today bestselling author of the epic fantasy series THE SORCERER'S RING, comprising seventeen books; of the #1 bestselling series THE VAMPIRE JOURNALS, comprising twelve books; of the #1 bestselling series THE SURVIVAL TRILOGY, a post-apocalyptic thriller comprising three books; of the epic fantasy series KINGS AND SORCERERS, comprising six books; of the epic fantasy series OF CROWNS AND GLORY, comprising 8 books; of the epic fantasy series A THRONE FOR SISTERS, comprising seven books (and counting); and of the new science fiction series THE INVASION CHRONICLES. Morgan's books are available in audio and print editions, and translations are available in over 25 languages.

Morgan loves to hear from you, so please feel free to visit www.morganricebooks.com to join the email list, receive a free book, receive free giveaways, download the free app, get the latest exclusive news, connect on Facebook and Twitter, and stay in touch!

Made in the USA
Las Vegas, NV
22 February 2022